Praise for Eli: *Greatness Continues*

"In *Eli*, we read how God can be glorified in greatness; in *Eli: Greatness Continues*, we read how God can be glorified in suffering. The problem of pain and sin is grappled in many pages of this book, with the aim of confident trust in God through all things reaching out to touch the reader's heart."

—David Norland, pastor of New Life
Lutheran Church, LCMC

"This book is amazing! I really like the thought that God watches everything with Peter and sends angels like little Thumbnail to watch out for us. It made me want to listen harder for what God wants me to do. It's neat to watch how Eli handles these situations and then how God reacts. It shows sadness, but also how God is taking care of everything."

—Alli Webber (Age 14)

TO MY FRIEND
TONI

ELI.
-GREATNESS CONTINUES-

Be Blessed

-GREATNESS CONTINUES-

MICHAEL D. GOLDSMITH

TATE PUBLISHING
AND ENTERPRISES, LLC

Published by Tate Publishing & Enterprises, LLC
127 E. Trade Center Terrace | Mustang, Oklahoma 73064 USA
1.888.361.9473 | www.tatepublishing.com

Tate Publishing is committed to excellence in the publishing industry. The company reflects the philosophy established by the founders, based on Psalm 68:11,

"The Lord gave the word and great was the company of those who published it."

Book design copyright © 2015 by Tate Publishing, LLC. All rights reserved.
Cover design by Roland Caballero
Interior design by Manolito Bastasa

Published in the United States of America

ISBN: 978-1-68118-733-4
Fiction / Religious
15.08.14

Eli: Greatness Continues is the second labor of love God our Father has had me do. I would like to dedicate this work to the third most important loves in my life.

To my kids: Rebecca, Michelle, Rachael, and Jonathon Michael, and the great-grandkids they have provided me. Rebecca's four are Samuel, Aaron, Leah, and Ryan. Michelle's three are Eli, Anya, and Soren. Rachael's Avayla, Jonathon's Erica and Eddie.

Kids, I hope you enjoy reading this as much as I did writing it.

Love,
Dad

Contents

• • • • • • •

1

The Last Inning Is the New Beginning

ELI STOOD ON the mound looking down at Rucket. His shoulder was throbbing. The first two pitches had taken their toll. He threw, and the ball was so fast it could barely be seen. Rucket fanned it. He was out.

As Rucket fanned it, the pain Eli felt just about drove him to his knees. He looked to the stands, saw that his mom and Jill were sitting together, praying. He smiled and prayed.

"Father, just get me through this inning."

He was able to finesse his way around the next two batters. He got them each out on three pitches. The pain was intense. LA won the series. As Eli looked around the stadium, he knew in his heart that was it. Now it was time to reach the kids. But, according to his contract, he had to let the doctors decide his fate.

Eli remained on the mound, the pain intense; the crowd was roaring with their excitement. LA had just won the

World Series. His team knew to hold back and not rush out as they could see Eli was in intense pain. But even in the pain, Eli was taking in the crowd. He could smell the scents of the stadium. He could feel the absolute joy the crowd was experiencing. No one could understand why the team was not rushing Eli to hoist him up on their shoulders. The crowd sensed there was something terribly wrong. He looked up into the stands and saw the sweet face of his bride, Jill. He knew this part of his life was over, and he knew the work ahead would not be easy. He turned 360 degrees on the mound. He took in the sights and sounds of the greatness Father had given him as a ball player for the last time.

His teammate and close friend, Sam Boursa, walked up to him and asked, "Eli, you okay man?"

"Sam, there is nothing left. The arm is shot. Maybe my grandpa was right when I was ten, as he told me that I was working too hard, but you know what? God is in control. It's time to reach the kids," Eli said.

Eli walked off the field for the last time and into the locker room, called Dr. Jones over, and asked him look at his shoulder. The pain was like nothing Eli had ever felt before in his life. Even the pain of straightening his hips when he was ten didn't come close to the pain that he felt in his shoulder. The doc took him in and did an MRI in the team's medical center.

"Eli, it does not look good. I am going to send you over to UCIA to see what they can do with the shoulder, but I don't have great hopes for this," the doctor said.

The next day Eli saw Morton Smith, the best orthopedic doctor in the state. After what seemed like hours, and after many tests, Dr. Smith came back into the room.

"Mr. McBrien, I think we are going to have to do surgery. Even with that, I don't know what we can do to fix it. We may be able to make the pain go away, but your pitching days may be over," the doctor stated with great concern.

⚾ ⚾ ⚾

"Father, can you do something, can you fix that shoulder so he can pitch again?" Pete asked.

"Pete, you know I can, but that does not fit my plan. I created Eli for the purpose of reaching kids. Next year, he will have enough fame to go into the ghetto and start working with the kids. My plan will work. It always does," was the gentle reply from the great I Am.

"When I put Eli and Jill together, it was for this purpose, and yes, his team will be winners as well," continued the Father in his loving voice.

⚾ ⚾ ⚾

Eli looked at the doc and then to Jill and then back at the doc. "When can we do the surgery?" he asked.

"How's next week sound?" the doctor replied.

In the usual way he stated, "Let's git 'er dun."

Eli and Jill decided to take a cruise with Sam and Corrine during the week in between the season end and the surgery. They spent hours walking on the upper deck by the pool. Eli would put his arm around his sweet wife.

He smiled and just enjoyed the quiet and the sound of the water going by the ship as they sailed the Caribbean. A totally relaxed Eli looked at Jill. "You know, hun, I would love to play again, but I am beginning to think Father has other plans for me. I really love the game, but I feel drawn in another direction."

Jill looked at Eli. Her big blue eyes had a little tear in them. Then a flash of brilliance raced across her mind.

"See, Pete, the idea of new beginnings is going to come through a great woman, much like when I asked Mary to carry my Son and bring him into the world to bring a new beginning to mankind," the Father said.

Eli and Jill's cruise ended, and so did their short week of relaxation. The time seemed so short, but they both knew the job ahead of them was a major undertaking.

"Eli, what would happen if you took those gang members from Watts and turned them into a great amateur baseball team? I think you could do a lot with them," Jill said, with that sly grin on her face that only came out when her ideas truly had a great brilliance to them. "Imagine how you could speak into their lives!" Eli's beautiful bride said.

"Jill, that's brilliant," Eli responded as he put his arms around his wife and pulled her close to him. "What would I do without you?"

Jill got a sly grin across her lips. "You better never try to find out, mister," she said.

As they walked into their condo, Eli noticed his guitar sitting in the corner. He picked it up to practice his runs. Jill's eyes still got big.

"Sweetheart, I have listened to you a thousand times. I knew you were good, but it seems that our Father, through his Son, by his Spirit, has added something new to your playing. There is something different in the tone and the way you run the chords. You were good before, Eli, you're great! How long has it been since you have played it, hun?"

Eli smiled then winked at his sweet bride. "Babes, I just feel totally filled with the Spirit himself tonight. It's like I am not playing this instrument myself, but it is the Father's Spirit playing through me, if that makes sense at all." Eli got up from his chair, walked over, and set his guitar down and said, "I could play all night. But it's time to get to work."

As they were walking around their condo for the first time in a week, Eli and Jill started prep work on what would be an adventure that would last the rest of their lives.

"Pete, remember when he played for the youth group and I told you his music would be part of his greatness? Just watch this," the Father said.

Eli once again used his tuner to bring the guitar back into tune. He turned up his amp to a level where it would almost knock out windows and decided to play "Secret Ambition," his theme song whenever he was on the mound.

As he was playing, he could almost hear the drums. Then it hit his mind like a ray of lightning, the secret ambition. The drive, he could see the kids in Watts. He knew he had to touch the kids.

As Eli grabbed his cell phone, Jill said, "Eli, who are you calling this late at night?"

"I am going to call Sam. He plays drums. I'll have him call Jack Thomas from the Heat. He's here all winter, and I know he is a Christian and a great bass player. I think we can have this band put together in a week," Eli stated with an excitement that touched Jill to the core.

Eli called Sam.

"Hey buddy, I've got a great idea! Let's get a hold of Mack and put together a band to reach these kids."

"Eli, I know Lou Johnson. She is a great keyboard player," stated Sam.

The next day Sam was on the phone. Eli was standing right beside him.

"Eli, I have decided that what we are doing here is more important than baseball. I am leaving the team," Sam said, surprising everyone in the room.

"Sam, you have many good years ahead of you. Are you sure you want to do this? The money you could earn would be millions," Eli said.

"Look, Eli, there is a call on us. God put us together for a reason, and baseball was part of it but for a short season.

Baseball will be it for a long time but not professionally. Can you imagine the squeeze play these guys could pull off?" Sam responded.

"Sam, when I think what we can do with music and the rhythm it produces, it will have as great an impact on teaching them the game of baseball." Then Eli did another run with his guitar. Eli's ability to use his fingers running up and down the neck of his guitar was equaled only by his pitching ability.

As he continued the runs, Jill began to dance. She was showing off her dance moves and smiling at her husband. Eli looked up to heaven and mouthed, "Thank you!"

⚾ ⚾ ⚾

"Father, how will you protect them when they go into the ghetto?" Pete asked.

The look God gave Peter could have melted a mountain, "Ah, Pete, who am I?"

"Father, let me rephrase that. Who are you going to use to protect them?"

"How does Thumbnail sound?" the great I Am responded.

"Father, I realize, that at times, I may be dense, but Thumbnail?" Pete asked totally dumbfounded.

"Pete, stay tuned. You are in for some surprises," the Father stated with a soft chuckle and grin.

⚾ ⚾ ⚾

It was Monday of the following week. Eli walked into Memorial Hospital in Los Angeles.

The nurse smiled at him, "Eli McBrien, we have been expecting you. We have a bunch of tests to run on you today, and we'll get you a good night's sleep tonight, and surgery is in the morning."

Eli smiled, knowing that his shoulder pain would be diminished, but that his days on the mound were over.

In his room, the phone rang. "Hi, this is Eli."

"Eli, this is Aaron Boursa. How are you?"

"Aaron, are you related to Sam?"

"Yeah! He's my cousin. Never told you, ha?"

"Can't say that he did, or you for that matter," Eli answered.

"I am a senior this year. I've been having a good year. Not the pitcher that you were, but doing okay. I am headed to LA next year. Sam said I could live with them while I work on my teaching degree. I want to go into coaching," Aaron stated, with pride of accomplishment in his voice.

Eli responded with confidence and excitement. "Aaron, I am so impressed with you. To think that you were able to overcome the entire negative experience and all the put-downs plus become a decent pitcher makes me so proud. Aaron, as you know, I am in the hospital right now. They are going to see what they can do with this shoulder. What has Sam shared with you about what is going on?" Eli asked.

"Eli, pretty much that you think your pitching days are over. Will the surgery help with the pain?"

"Yeah, bud, but it's the second time in my life I have been under a surgeon's knife. The first time was not fun. I don't expect this to be much better."

The nurse came into the room. "Mr. McBrien, it's time." They rolled Eli down to the operating room. He looked across the table, and to his surprise he saw Dr. Thomas, the doctor who had worked on his hips when he was only ten years old.

"Eli, I heard that you were going to have this surgery. Your doctor here is one of the best. I have asked him if I could observe the surgery. I have looked at the X-rays, which he e-mailed to me, and asked him if I could scrub in. Don't know if I will be needed at all, but I just wanted to be here," Dr. Thomas said.

Eli, feeling more and more groggy from the drugs, answered, "Doctor Thomas, I am glad you're here. I felt I was in great hands before. Now I know I really am. Thank you for coming. Docs, let's get 'er done," Eli stated in his immutable fashion.

Six hours later, the nurse woke Eli. His shoulder was in a cast, totally immobilized.

Eli's vision was blurry. He blinked his eyes a few times and focused on his lovely wife. To her side was another person, Aaron Boursa.

"Aaron, how did you get here so quickly?"

"Eli, I flew in yesterday and am already moved in with Sam and Corrine. I was able to graduate with a 3.5 GPA from high school. I did everything that I needed to do as a ball player. And it all started with one game with you in Minneapolis," Aaron said.

Eli smiled as he said, "Aaron, you have shown me a couple of things. One is your love of the game. The second thing is that you're smart. As a coach, you have to be able to read situations that can make or break a game. That takes a lot of brains. You have to be able to outthink the other coach. That takes planning. It is also important that everything you do on the field, with your players, draws them to the Father. That, my friend, is wisdom. I really think that you have all three."

Aaron's face was turning just a bit red from all the positive feedback he was getting from Eli. "Eli, your confidence in me is exactly what I need to be able to reach the kids our Father in heaven is going to bring across our path. I just had to stop by and see you, bud. I will stop by again later." With that, Aaron left.

"Give me a call!" Eli said as Aaron left the room.

"You got it!" Aaron replied.

"Eli McBrien, I am so much in love with you. To think about what you did for Aaron was nothing short of a miracle. You have brought him so far." Jill said in a loving tone that showed the love and caring she had for the one Father chose for her.

Eli smiled, put his hand on hers, squeezed a little, turned his head, and kissed her lightly. "Babes, I love you too. It was not me, it was Christ."

The doctor walked into the room. "Mr. McBrien, I have some good news and some bad news." Jill walked up behind Eli, and Eli put her arms around his neck.

Eli responded, "Give me the good news first."

"The operation was a success. The pain should be gone in your shoulder."

"And the bad news?" Eli requested.

"Your joint was pretty much shot. If you try to pitch again, we would have to put a new shoulder joint in by mid-season."

"Doc, if we put a new shoulder in would I be able to pitch?" Never really wanting to quit Eli asked.

"Not a chance." Was the extremely quick response.

"How long will I not be able to use the shoulder?"

The doctor's answer came just as quickly. "About three weeks."

"We are going to keep you overnight. You can go home in the morning." With that, the doctor left.

Eli and Jill spent the next several hours talking about the plans the great I Am had laid on their hearts to help the kids from Watts. The excitement the Father had placed on their hearts for this mission would be the driving force behind many of the events that would happen in the next few years of their life together. As the hour grew late, Jill kissed Eli good night and drove the short distance home. She would return the next morning.

🏐 🏐 🏐

Early the next morning, Eli was released. He walked out and saw the Challenger. Jill was standing beside it with a little grin on her face.

"You are going to take it easy on the way home, are you not?" Eli asked.

Jill responded with a wink, "Eli, would I drive less than totally civil in your precious car?"

"I don't know, you tell me," Eli responded.

Eli slid into the passenger side of the Challenger, a spot he had only been in once. Eli had purchased Jill a more sedate, Lincoln Continental.

Eli looked over at Jill who had a sly grin on her face he had never seen before.

"I have been waiting a long time for this," she said with a giggle that sent shivers up and down Eli's spine. Then she turned the key. The Hemi jumped to life, and she slammed her foot to the floor. The G forces slammed Eli back in his seat. She looked in her rearview mirror and saw the blue smoke coming from the radials and heard the squelch of the tires, as the Challenger jumped out from under her. "Eli, this is AweSOME!" she squealed like a little girl. Just then, the lights of the squad car came on behind her.

"Nooo!" Jill said. She pulled the Challenger over and dropped her head onto the steering wheel.

The officer came to her window. He looked inside the car and recognized Eli. "Aren't you Eli McBrien?" he asked.

"Yes, officer, just going home from the hospital," Eli stated.

"I take it you are Mrs. McBrien?" the officer asked.

Jill's head was still resting on the steering wheel. She did not lift it. "Yes, officer, that's me."

"Mrs. McBrien, what's the hurry?" was the officer's quick request.

Raising her head a little, she said, "Eli never lets me drive this car. He says that it has way too much power for me. So when I had to pick him up from the hospital today, I thought I would drive it and show him I could handle it.

So when we left the hospital, I thought I would have some fun. So I stomped on it to see what would happen."

The officer got a big smile on his face. "You found out, did you not?"

"Yes!" was the sheepish answer from Jill.

"Mrs. McBrien, let's be careful."

"Yes, officer. Absolutely!" Jill said, almost crying.

The rest of the trip home, she drove very carefully.

As they arrived at their condo, Jill made sure Eli got into the condo without a problem. They spent the rest of the day around the pool. Eli leaned back on the lounge, looked at his beautiful wife, and realized that God had put him into the great situation that he was in now.

⚾ ⚾ ⚾

"Father, what are you going to be doing with Eli now?" Pete asked.

"Pete, just watch. The best is yet to come," the Father of all mankind answered.

⚾ ⚾ ⚾

It had been three weeks. Eli was getting to the point where he could do more things around the house. It was Saturday morning. As was his custom when he was in the off-season, he would make breakfast for his bride. He had the tray set up with a flower in a small vase, coffee, toast, bacon, and eggs.

As he walked in, Jill rubbed the sleep from her eyes. "Eli, you make me love you more every day," Jill said, smiling.

Eli responded with a sly grin, "I know."

While Jill enjoyed her breakfast, Eli excused himself and walked to the bathroom. He jumped into the shower, feeling the warm water flow over him, invigorating his senses. He said a special prayer of thanks for the new waterproof material they made casts out of these days. He dressed quickly in shorts and a T-shirt then walked out of the bathroom. Just then, he heard a knock on the door.

"Morning, Sam, what's up?" Eli said.

"It's Jamaal. He's gotten himself into some real trouble."

"What did he do?"

"Eli, he got involved in a gang war. He is in the hospital," was Sam's frantic answer.

Eli ran back to his bedroom. Jill was already up putting on her robe.

"Eli, get going! You have to get to the hospital, now! God is using you to touch him, get going."

Eli gave his bride a hug and a kiss then headed out with Sam to the hospital.

Sam and Eli entered the parking lot in Sam's BMW. They parked and got to the hospital as quickly as possible without hurting Eli's shoulder.

Sam ran up to the desk and asked where Jamaal's room was.

They explained that they were Eli McBrien and Sam Boursa; that they had both retired so they could build the new baseball league so these gang wars could be put to a stop. Then they explained that Jamaal was going to be part of the league.

They were sent to the Intensive Care Unit.

Jamaal looked at Eli and smiled through his bruised lips. "Eli, with that shoulder in a harness, I wonder who is in worse shape."

Eli, shaking his head, answered, "Jamaal, mine was planned. You have a bright future, if you let the Father control your life."

"Eli, they called us out. They challenged us. When we are challenged, we meet it," Jamaal responded.

Eli had a light bulb light up his brain. "They want a challenge? Fine, let's get them on a baseball diamond."

⚾ ⚾ ⚾

"Pete, watch what I do here with Eli and Sam," the Alpha and Omega stated majestically.

⚾ ⚾ ⚾

Eli looked at Sam and said, "It's time we show them constructive use of their competitive nature."

Sam responded, "I think we need to start getting that new baseball league off the ground."

"I think we should put the challenge out to all the gangs. They can show just how good they really are…by playing baseball."

2
Meeting the Challenge

SATURDAY NIGHT, ELI and Jill were walking out of mass. Father Mike was greeting people as they were walking out of the door. "Eli, it's good to see you. I heard you're starting a new Protestant church in Watts?" Father Mike asked.

Eli got a puzzled look on his face. "Father, that's correct, but how did you hear about it?"

"Stuart Johnson is a friend of mine. We were undergrad classmates. You don't know this, but he started out to be a priest as well. We both became active in the charismatic renewal in the church. We both got 'filled' with the Holy Spirit at the same time. He felt God's call away from the Catholic Church, but we stayed in close contact," Father Mike stated.

"What he is doing in Watts will draw many from this body in. I realized that we rejected your vision to begin with, but there are people here who will still catch it," Father Mike continued. "Please stay in contact with me going forward. We will be more than happy to assist anyway we can." Father Mike finished.

"Thank you so much Father. I am sure there will be times when those young men who played Bible Baseball with us would love to come to a game and see those guys play. Maybe a little competition of real baseball?" Eli said with a sly grin.

Eli looked over at Jill. She was starting to hop up and down. The excitement in her eyes brought a smile to Eli's face. He knew in his heart that Jill was totally on board with what Father was placing on their hearts, to reach these kids that were before this time given up on by society.

⚾ ⚾ ⚾

"Pete, I am going to reach hundreds of kids by using these guys that I have planted my vision in. Remember when I told you that Eli would always give me the glory? Now you are seeing it."

⚾ ⚾ ⚾

As Eli and Jill walked over to the Challenger, Jill got a little grin on her face.

"Eli, I have been thinking."

"Yeah, Babes, what is it?"

"I thought we might just need a bigger car."

"What do you mean, sweetheart? This car is fine. It still gives me a rush when I hit the pedal."

"Eli, you have had this car since you were seventeen. It's getting a lot of miles on it, and it's going to be difficult to put the baby seat in the back."

Eli got a stunned look on his face. "B-b-baby seat?" he stammered.

"Yeah, sweetheart!" Jill said with that sly grin of hers.

"Jill, you're…"

"Yes, Eli, you're going to be a father. You will meet our child in eight months. And no I am not pregnant. We are."

"Wow!" was the only response he could muster.

With that, Eli looked at Jill and said, "Wait a minute. You already drive a Lincoln. Why do I have to give up my car?"

Jill simply smiled.

⚾ ⚾ ⚾

"Father, is this going to be a point of conflict for them?" asked Pete.

"Pete, not a chance. It was being used by Jill as a point of just telling him about the new life that I am creating here."

⚾ ⚾ ⚾

Eli called Sam. "Hey buddy, I have some great news. Jill is expecting."

Sam chuckled, "What? Wow! Corrine and I would love to be. Congrats, man."

Eli asked, "What about the team?"

"Eli, you're going to be a father to a number of guys that you coach through your life! You are also going to have a son or daughter that will be born for you to raise up into the kingdom, and baseball will be part of their upbringing. Suppose we should take a drive down and share our great news that the team that Father is going to build will have a bat boy/girl soon?"

"That is probably a good idea," Eli answered. "We have a lot of work in front of us. Remind me that I have to contact the City League to find out what we have to do to get this team into the league."

Sam asked, "Meet you there?"

"Sounds great! Be there in ten." And hung up.

Eli walked over to Jill.

"Hun, we are going to go down to Watts to do some work with the boys. Wanna come with? Their girlfriends could probably use some 'coaching' as well," Eli said.

Jill, smiling, looked at Eli, "Better call Sam and tell him to bring Corrine."

Eli grabbed his phone and hit speed dial, "Sam, Jill is coming with. Can you bring Corrine?"

"Buddy, I'm already on my way. You should have called sooner."

"That's okay, I'll pass it on to Jill."

"I figured you would ask your bride, and if you had not, we were going to recruit her to come with as well."

"So you're bringing Corrine, I take it?"

"You got it, bro. We have a ton of work ahead of us, so let's get rolling."

Sam and Corrine arrived at Eli and Jill's in ten minutes flat.

As they walked out, Eli opened the door for Jill, and she got into the back of Sam and Corrine's BMW SUV.

"Eli, you made about $130 million last year with LA, didn't you?"

"Yeah, that's what I took home. I made closer to two hundred million. Uncle Sam took the rest."

"How much did you end up with in the bank?"

"I have about a hundred million left."

"And you guys are expecting a baby right?"

"That's right," Eli stated in a disgruntled voice.

"And your little sister, Leah, is now attending school in Colorado is that correct?"

"Yeah, Dad is paying big bucks for her education."

Sam got a smile on his face. "Does she have a car?"

"No. Your point?" Eli responded.

"Why don't you give her the Challenger and buy something that will work better for the baby?"

Eli just shook his head.

"Look, Eli, besides our children, which are the best gift Father could give us, we are going to have to drive these teams around."

Eli started thinking to himself, *That makes sense, and Lea will love this car. The only real problem is the power. If I am going to help her with a car, I think I could just buy her something sporty with a whole lot less power.*

As they drove into Watts, some gangs started to surround the BMW.

Jamaal came out with his boys. Jamaal, in a voice that rung out with authority, yelled at the other gang members, "You guys back off! These are friends of ours, and no harm will come to them!"

The anger welled up inside the opposing gang member. "How you gonna stop us?" was yelled back at them.

The battle began as Sam slammed the BMW into reverse and got out of there.

One of the opposing gang members was about to hit Jamaal with a huge pipe, Jamaal ducked and caught the pipe in the ribs, breaking three of them. As he bent over in pain, he was struck in the back with the same pipe, which drove him to the ground. With blood pouring out of his mouth and nose, he managed to barely say "Help me!" The rival gang ran off. Someone called an ambulance. Jamaal was taken back to the hospital.

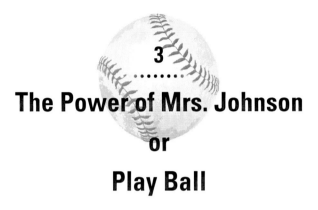

3
The Power of Mrs. Johnson
or
Play Ball

IT HAD BEEN three weeks, and Jamaal was finally ready to get out of the hospital. Eli's arm was out of his sling, but he still could not move his shoulder very well.

As Eli and Sam were making their way to the hospital to pick up Jamaal, they saw him walking out with his mother. She was shaking her finger at him.

"Listen here, tough boy. If you ever, I mean ever, get involved with that gang again, they won't have to kill you, I will!" Jamaal Johnson, the big tough Watts gang king was brought to his knees by his mama!

● ● ●

Pete, with a grin on his face, said, "Father, when you made moms, you gave them some real power, didn't you?"

"Pete, you have no idea. The power of a mom is beyond anything that you could ever imagine."

Eli and Sam walked up to Jamaal's mom.

Sam let out a slightly raised voice and got their attention.

"Mrs. Johnson? Sam Boursa here. Can we give you folks a ride home?" he asked.

Eleanor Johnson got a surprised look on her face.

"Are you the same Sam Boursa that played for the baseball team?"

"I am," he answered quickly. "I have retired so I can work with the kids in the ghetto."

Eli grinned and said, "Mrs. Johnson, we have in mind to start a baseball team with these guys. I think Jamaal will make a fine ball player."

Jamaal, with a quizzical look on his face, said, "Eli, what makes you think I would be a ball player of any kind?"

"Jamaal, you're quick, you're resourceful, and you hate to lose. I have seen ball players in the pros who don't hate to lose as much as you do. What we have to be able to do is take that desire to win and put it to constructive use."

The look on Jamaal's face was priceless! Even the bright California sunshine was not as bright as the smile on Jamaal's face. The desire to accomplish great things had always been on his mind. However, he had never thought anything could come his way that would be anything greater than being a gang leader. He was about to find out that great things come from the great I Am, the Creator of greatness Himself.

The Father looked over to Pete and said, "Pete, I am going to take this young man and turn him into a great hitter. Eli is going to be a huge influence, but I have it in mind for Aaron to be the coach that can get his self-confidence to where he needs it to be. Remember years ago when Eli took him to a ball game? Well, that was the start of Aaron becoming the great coach that I created him to be."

Jamaal was still sore from the beating he took. "Mom, can these guys please give us a ride home?" he asked.

Eleanor nodded. Both Jamaal and his mom got in the back of Sam's BMW.

Eli looked over at Sam. "Can you drop me by my place? It's on the way to Jamaal's, and Jill is going to have supper for me."

After dropping off Eli, Sam turned to Jamaal. "Dude, are you ready to change your life and the lives of your friends?"

Jamaal blinked as he said, "What do you mean change my life and my friends?"

Sam got a smile on his face. "Jamaal, your gang wants to control the whole ghetto, right?"

The answer to that question came quickly. "Yeah!"

"Then let's do it with baseball", was Sam's response.

Jamaal shook his head. "Man, I hope you're a good salesman."

Sam smiled. "The Guy who leads me every day is the best. He created sales."

Shaking his head in disbelief, Jamaal said, "Boy, he better be because this ain't gonna be easy."

Arriving at their home, Sam dropped off Jamaal and his mom. Then he turned his car toward the nice part of town he and Corrine lived in.

⚾ ⚾ ⚾

Eli picked up the phone and dialed Sam. "Hey Sam, I think it's time to start our team."

Sounding surprised, Sam responded, "What team?"

Eli, shaking his head, responded, "You know how we talked about these guys would be a great team? It's time to start it."

Sam with a chuckle said, "Eli, I am just pulling your chain. I agree. It's time. I just dropped Jamaal off. I ran the idea by him, and the only thing he could say was, 'Man, I hope you're a good salesman.' I told him that we work for the best."

"Okay, Sam, let's git 'er dun," was the quick response from Eli.

Sam walked into the kitchen where Corinne was making supper. He walked up behind her, put his arms around her tiny waste, and could feel the womb that would one day soon be the home for the first nine months of his child's life. He gave her a light kiss on her neck and said, "Well, babes, we are going to start a team. I really do think we should see if Aaron is interested in helping with the coaching."

Sam picked up the phone and called Eli. "Hey bud, what do you say we get Aaron involved with the coaching?"

Eli, with a chuckle, responded, "I was just thinking the same thing. Let's do a quick conference call."

◌ ◌ ◌

Looking over at Pete, Father smiled. "Pete, this is going to be good. Aaron is going to be really stoked about this."

◌ ◌ ◌

"Aaron, it's your cousin, Sam, and our best bud Eli. We have a great idea. I think it's a God thing." Before Sam could finish, Aaron said, "You guys are gonna start a ball team with the guys in the ghetto, aren't you?"

Sam's jaw dropped. "How did you ever figure that out?"

"Sam, it was just a natural chain of events. I know the two of you had been working with these guys. You know I have been in school for coaching, and I need the credits."

Eli piped in. "You need the credits?"

Aaron shook his head, "Yeah, I can set up an independent study coaching your team. It could really make my job getting everything lined up easier."

◌ ◌ ◌

Jamaal walked into his gang headquarters, looked around, saw Lucia sitting in a chair.

"Lucia, what are you doing here this time of day?" the question came quickly.

"Jamaal, there is trouble in the pit."

The look on Jamaal's face brought fear to Lucia's.

"What do you mean trouble in the pit?" Came the question in a voice that sounded almost satanic.

$$\cdot \quad \cdot \quad \cdot$$

"Father, what is going on here? What is the pit?"

The response that God gave Peter was so strong and authoritative that the walls of heaven shook.

"The pit is where the scumbags that have been destroying my kids for years keep their drugs that are so destructive. I have a special place in hell for the people who use my kids as slaves, just so they can make their money off of them."

"I have Mark Smith, who had been looking for the pit for two years. Suddenly by chance, "He thinks" walked right into the pit. Twenty-five of Jamaal's gang buddies went to jail."

$$\cdot \quad \cdot \quad \cdot$$

Thumbnail, sitting on Eli's shoulder, whispered in his ear. "Eli, you better call Jamaal. You will save his life."

Eli shrugged his shoulders, picked up his phone, and hit the speed dial. Jamaal answered.

"Hey buddy, what's going on? I really felt like I needed to call you."

The darkness that Jamaal thought was gone now returned and was transferred through the phone. The bright California sun was now not so bright. Jamaal realized the gravity of the situation he found himself in but had no clue how he was going to get out of this. He could see endless jail time staring him in the face, and he was scared. He got himself together so he could sound confident as he answered the question that Eli had asked.

"Eli, there is nothing going on. Just got into a little scrap with the law over some property I had hidden," Jamaal answered in a way that really got Eli's attention.

The look on Eli's face showed concern, older than his years. "Jamaal, what have you hidden?"

"Twenty-five kilos of meth," was his answer.

Eli's jaw dropped to the floor. "Meth?"

Jamaal continued, "They also have me in the death of a little red-headed boy."

Eli could hear the sobbing in Jamaal's voice.

"Yeah!" Eli simply said.

"Eli, they're taking me to jail!"

Thumbnail whispered to Eli, "Meet him there."

Eli called Jill, informed her about what was going on, and then called Sam.

"Sam, I just got off the phone with Jill. Jamaal really got himself into a heap of trouble on this one."

Sam answered quite baffled, "What do you mean?"

Eli answered "Drugs, Sam. Meth. It also appears they have him for selling meth to a 10 year old. The youngster died. I have no sympathy for him. Let him rot."

Sam shook his head, "Want me to go to the station with you? But know this. God brought us into Jamaal's life. He knew about this from the start. We cannot give up on him."

"Sam that would be great! I will pick you up in ten."

Eli walked out of the apartment, looked at his new Cadillac, and hopped in, started it up, headed out of the driveway, thinking to himself, *The Challenger was a lot more fun to drive.*

A few minutes later, Eli pulled up to Sam's new house. He drove up the circular driveway in front of the new house Sam had just purchased for his bride and himself. Sam walked out, kissed Corrine, and hopped in the Caddy beside Eli.

As they were driving, Eli looked over to Sam and said, "Somehow, mercy is not what I am feeling toward Jamaal right now. I could wring his neck."

Sam's answer was in an instant. "Bud, I am sure that is what God the Father through His Son by His Spirit feels sometimes when we mess up as well. Just remember that when we meet with Jamaal."

◊ ◊ ◊

Peter looked over at the Father, "Are you going to destroy Jamaal for hurting your kids?"

Father responded as only he could, "No, Pete. I am going to destroy those who, by their greed, enticed Jamaal into such a life and refused to repent. If they will call on the name of my Son, Jesus, they all can be saved. However, if they continue to live their lives destroying my kids, their destruction is on their heads. Then I will use Jamaal to rebuild the lives of other kids and bring more of them into my kingdom."

As they arrived at the station, thumbnail whispered to Eli, "You will get him mercy, but not without cost. He must be disciplined for what he has done to Father's kids. But it's not too late for redemption for him."

Eli and Sam walked up to the desk sergeant, a pretty lady, fit, but totally business like. "May I help you?" was the question that was totally expected.

Eli talked to the sergeant. "Ma'am, I am Eli McBrien. May I see Jamaal?"

Curtly, the sergeant snapped, "And what, may I ask, do you have to do with that dredge of the earth?"

Eli replied with a bit of disgust, "Do you know who I am?"

"No, Mister McBrien, I do not. And I don't really care. Now can you tell me what you have to do with Jamaal?"

Eli shook his head in disbelief. "Sergeant, did you see any of the World Series last year?"

The desk sergeant got a reddish embarrassment color to her face as she realized just who Eli really was. "Yes, I did, and now I know who you are. Could I get your autograph for my husband?"

"Do I get to see Jamaal?" was Eli's immediate response.

"Mr. McBrien, if that's what it will take, then you got it." She called and told them to bring Jamaal up to see them in the visiting room.

"Mr. McBrien, how about that autograph?" came the question from the desk sergeant.

Eli quickly grabbed a piece of paper, wrote how blessed the guy was to have such a great wife, and signed it "Eli McBrien, Los Angeles."

As Eli and Sam walked toward the visiting room, Sam whispered to Eli, "You sure know how to get the most out of your fame, don't you?"

Eli gave a little chuckle. "Remember when Paul was going to be struck by one of the leaders of the Jews in the book of Acts. He pulled his Roman citizenship out. I learned my lessons well." Eli just smiled as they waited for Jamaal.

Five minutes later Jamaal came in, looked at Eli and Sam, and started to cry.

"Man, I forgot about those drugs. When Christ changed me, I had intended to destroy those drugs. Before I could go to the pit, it got raided. Now what do I do?" The redness in Jamaal's eyes was telling of the remorse he was feeling.

Eli got up off of his chair and started to pace the room. Back and forth he walked, pounding his fist on the desk. "Jamaal! Are you crying because you're truly remorseful or because you got caught?

"Jamaal, there is another problem we have to deal with. What about the little red-headed boy. Did you give him the meth?" Eli asked Jamaal angrily. Eli looked over at Sam, and Sam at Eli. Shaking his head, he told Sam, "We can't ask him anything, if we do, and he tells us, then we are able to be questioned in court."

Jamaal volunteered. "I am going to confess. I did it. I killed him. Can you guys help me get mercy?"

Sam got a concerned look on his face. "Have your attorney contact us. We will have to see just what has to be done and if there is anything that can be done. But to be honest I don't feel a lot of mercy in me right now."

"Jamaal, do you realize how many lives you have destroyed by selling those drugs? Just think of the little red-headed boy. This little guy was his mom and dad's pride and joy. You killed him. You took the future God had planned for him and snuffed it out. How dare you. Jamaal, to be honest, I would have no problem pushing the needle into your arm and sending the killing juice into you myself. Watching you cough and gag on the table would not bother me a bit," Eli said.

Then Eli asked, "How old were the kids you were selling to?" knowing the answer before he asked the question.

Jamaal got a look on his face that would scare a ghost. "Ten."

Eli's face turned red with anger. "If it were up to me, I would send you away for the rest of your life! My kid sister is ten," Eli yelled.

Sam pulled Eli aside, "There is redemption, and he has saved our skin more than once in the ghetto. Christ has changed him. Now is the time for him to take steps to help some of these kids he screwed up."

Eli walked over to Jamaal. "Look, I don't have a lot of mercy in me for what you have done to those innocent kids. I will talk to your attorney and then to the DA and see what we can arrange. For some reason, God is seeing fit to give you a break, maybe. But you're going to have to do some serious stuff to walk on this one."

With that, Eli and Sam walked out to the Caddy and went home to their wives.

The next morning both men were called by Jamaal's attorney, "I hear you and Sam are friends of Jamaal?"

Eli answered, "That's right, what can we do for yah?"

Reggie Somohato, Jamaal's attorney answered, "Jamaal is facing 150 years on the counts that they have on him. The kids he sold to are going to testify, except for the little red-headed boy that died of course. His mother will do the damage with that. It's going to be hard to get much mercy for him."

◊ ◊ ◊

Peter looked over at the Father and asked, "How are you going to save Jamaal on this one?"

"Pete, it's like this, I am going to touch the judge's heart, and I am going to use Eli to do it. But I am not going to get him off scot-free. That would be unjust. He will pay for what he has done, both now and after."

"After?" was the one-word question Peter asked the Father.

"Pete, some things are better for you not to know," the Father stated in a matter-of-fact tone.

◊ ◊ ◊

Eli and Sam arrived at Reggie's office to talk about the case.

Eli looked at Reggie and said, "Jamaal has to serve some tough time for what he has done. Here is what I am going to recommend to the judge. Jamaal gets 150 years,

140 of it is suspended, ten years to be served in the county jail. He will play baseball and work with the kids in his neighborhood to keep them off drugs. He will tell them that he is presently serving a sentence for the drug use and that if he is not playing ball with the guys from the ghetto and giving these talks, then he is in jail, and States' evidence to bust the rest of the scum of the earth."

Reggie got a look on his face that said, "This might work." Reggie said to Eli and Sam, "Are you guys willing to take some responsibility in this?"

Eli looked over at Sam, who nodded at Eli. Sam stated, "Look, I think we have something here that just might work. It's worth a try anyway."

With that, Reggie called the DA and ran the whole idea by him.

Franklin Wright, the district attorney, scratched his head and said, "Let me get this straight. You want me to agree to let this scum of garbage work with Eli McBrien and Sam Boursa while staying in jail to try to reach more kids and clean up the streets?"

Reggie responded. "Look, Frank, we have worked together on things for a long time to get kids off drugs. I hate what these guys do to kids as much as you do. Maybe the idea they have will work, maybe it won't. I think it's worth a try. If it works, we get some really bad suppliers. If it does not and Jamaal makes a break for it, you put him away forever. Why throw one more away. Besides, he turns state evidence, and you lock up a whole lot more scum."

Frank shook his head and took the idea to the county attorney (who knew Eli) and asked him. Lloyd James looked across his desk at Frank and said, "If Eli wants to give this a shot, okay. But make sure it's known that if Jamaal steps out of line even once, he goes away for the 150. With that provision, if he screws up even once, he still goes up."

Frank had only one provision to add to that. "Okay, let's do the lifetime probation. One stipulation I would add. After the ten years, the only thing considered a violation of probation is a felony. After all, he is putting his life on the line as it is by turning state's evidence."

Frank walked out, grabbed his phone, and called Reggie. "We have a deal. See what Jamaal says."

Back at his office, Reggie looked at Eli and Sam and said. "We have a deal. Jamaal steps out of line once, he goes to prison for the rest of his life. He stays in line for ten years, and he is free, except probation for life. Congrats, guys, you're now his parole officers."

Eli and Sam shook their heads, "Sam buddy, this is going to be an interesting run. I knew that we were going to be used but never had any idea it would be with this kind of stuff."

4
The Sentence

It was Monday, July 15. Jamaal had been called. He waived grand jury indictment and agreed to a plea bargain that Eli and Sam and Reggie had set up with the district attorney.

The plea bargain was for 150 years in prison, to be stayed for ten years in the county jail. He will play ball for the ghetto team and work with the neighborhood kids to keep them off drugs. Assuming he testifies against the drug lords who put him up to selling the drugs, his probation would be for life!

    ⚾ ⚾ ⚾

Pete looked to Father and asked, "How are you going to work this? You have just cuffed Eli and Sam's hands to Jamaal for ten years. How are you going to use this young man to touch other's lives when he has to be in jail every night for ten years?"

God the Father looked at Pete and just smiled, knowing exactly how he was going to work everything out. He turned to Peter and said, "Looks to me like the county jail is going to have a live-in chaplain for the next ten years. Besides playing ball and helping the other kids in the ghetto, Jamaal is going to be a huge help in building a Bible study in that jail that will go on forever."

Pete looked at the Father and said, "Father, you're going to get Aaron involved with the coaching. What kind of effect will he have on Jamaal, and what kind of effect will Jamaal have on the rest of the team?"

"Pete, what you're about to see will be the transformation, as only I can do it. Stay tuned and enjoy the ride."

Aaron knocked on Sam's door. "Hey Sam, what's this I hear about our job with the team getting even more challenging than we originally thought?"

Sam looked at Aaron. "You have not heard. Jamaal has messed up big time. We will have to spend a bunch of time later trying to explain it to you. Just know this. This is going to be a whole lot more time-consuming than we thought."

At this point, Eli stepped out from around the corner. Aaron asked Eli with a bit of excitement in his voice. "Eli man, do you still have the Challenger?"

Eli, with a bit of sadness in his voice said, "Nah, traded it in. Jill is having a baby, you know, and it's a girl. We thought about giving it to my little sister. We talked about just giving her the Challenger but decided it had way too much power for her. Remember Jill's little trick when she picked me up and got pulled over? Trading it in was my only option."

Just then the phone rang. "Hello, Eli here."

"Eli, this is Jamaal. What am I going to do? I get out for practice, for games, and to help with the kids keeping them off drugs."

Eli shook his head. "Hey dude! It's better than 150 years of hard time. Count your blessings and make the most of it. And remember this. You are also on probation for life. That means, if you ever, I mean ever, mess up, you go away."

Aaron grabbed the phone from Eli. "Jamaal, this is Aaron Boursa. Practice is tomorrow at 2:00 p.m. I will pick you up at one o'clock. Oh, by the way, when I heard Eli traded in his Challenger, I bought it."

Jamaal's voice got very excited. "Cool" was his only response.

Eli smiled as he told Aaron. "Hey dude, I hope they gave you a great deal."

"Nah" was the answer. "It was Sam who paid for it. I had to agree to a three-year contract coaching the team."

"Oh, by the way, Pastor Johnson called. He said he has ten other kids from the ghetto who want to play in the new church league."

🌑 🌑 🌑

In heaven there was a huge commotion. The angels were getting very active as Thumbnail got his second big assignment.

Gabriel called Thumbnail front and center.

"Thumbnail, I want to commend you on how well you have done with Eli over the last several years. So now Father has an even bigger assignment for you."

"Father wants you to sit on Jamaal's shoulder for the next ten years. You will be in jail with him. Your job will be to protect him, comfort him, and sing him to sleep at night. Do you think you can accomplish that?"

"Yes, sir!" was thumbnail's quick answer.

Father added, "Thumbnail, one other thing. Every night you will tell the little red-headed boy's mom that he still loves her, and she will see him again someday."

Thumbnail shrugged his shoulders and agreed. With that, Thumbnail was instantly on Jamaal's shoulder.

Peter looked puzzled as he asked the Father, "Thumbnail did a great job with Eli, how are you going to communicate with him now?"

"Pete, Eli is in a place now where when the quiet voice of my Spirit speaks to him, he hears it. Thumbnail is going to be much more useful working with Jamaal, where he is at in the jail, than with Eli," the Father answered.

The alarm rang. It was six thirty in the morning, and Jill walked past their bedroom where Eli was still sleeping. "Eli, it's time for you to get that cute butt of yours out of bed. You have a breakfast meeting with Sam then your press conference to announce the new baseball team, 'The Ghetto Giants.'"

Eli crawled out of bed, stumbled down the steps, kissed a very pregnant Jill on the forehead, and said, "You sure are beautiful this morning, sweetheart."

"Yeah, you tell me that all the time," Jill said softly in response, smiling broadly.

Eli took his first drink of coffee. "Man, this is good today."

Jill smiled, "It's a new one that Corrine told me about. I tried it at their house, thought you might like it."

"Sweetheart, it is really good this morning. You do know just what I need," Eli said as he took another sip of the premium roast.

With a smile on her face, Jill sweetly said, "Sweetheart, what's on your agenda today? Do you think that after your press conference that you will have time to take your sweet wife to look for some furniture for the baby's room?"

The smile on Eli's face was as broad as the lake of the woods back home in the north country of Minnesota. "Of course, Hun. Let's leave and grab some breakfast on the road." With that, they headed for the Caddy.

5
The Race for Life

Sam and Aaron walked into the jail. "We are here to see Jamaal," Aaron stated with confidence.

The guard walked back to get Jamaal from his cell. "Let's go, you have people wanting to see you."

Jamaal came out with his head down and shuffling his feet.

As he walked into the visiting room, Sam shook his head and said, "Jamaal, what kind of witness for Christ is that? You messed up big time. God, in his mercy, has you here with some opportunities to serve him and do a lot of good. All you seem to want to do is feel sorry for yourself. You could be in prison for the rest of your life. You know it and we know it. It's time to buck up and get to work."

The Father looked at Pete. "I have him just where I want him. When a person is conceived I give them all the gifts they will need for greatness in their lives. If they turn their hearts over to me and are willing to work hard, I can accomplish amazing things in their lives. They can however, by the use of my gifts, do things that are not what I would have them do. This young man is going to serve me just the way I need him to so that more lives can be changed," the Father said with a sly grin.

○ ○ ○

Jamaal looked across the table at Sam and Aaron. "When is our first practice?"

Sam spoke up quickly, "Next Monday at five thirty. Our first game is Wednesday at 6:00 p.m."

"We have twelve other guys from your hood ready to play. All you have to do is get your head out of your posterior and be ready to go. You mess this up, and I will see that you are sent away forever."

With that, Jamaal's countenance changed. His attitude was one of confidence, believing that he better start making a difference.

Jamaal replied, "Let's go to work."

Sam and Aaron could now see that Jamaal was ready to go to work and get the job done and be the leader that God the Father created him to be.

○ ○ ○

The Father looked at Pete and said, "Pete, now you're going to see what I can do with My wisdom and glory and power, plus My might. You're going to see one heart changed, which will lead to millions more being changed for my glory."

It was Monday at four thirty. Sam walked into the jail to get Jamaal. Jamaal came out in his red jumpsuit and cuffs. Sam shook his head. "How is he supposed to practice in that garb?"

Jamaal looked at Sam. "These are the only clothes I have here."

Sam grabbed his cell. "Eli, we need some practice clothes for Jamaal."

Eli responded, "The clothes will be at the park. I read the court order, he has to come cuffed and change here. When he works with the kids in the ghetto, he comes cuffed and in orange. This was designed to be an example of two things: One, what happens when you sell drugs to kids. Secondly, a warning to his boys from the hood who thought that what he had done was cool." Sam nodded as he spoke with Eli. He ended the call, looked at Jamaal, and said, "Let's go, champ, your workout clothes are at the park."

Jamaal got a curious look on his face. "What about the cuffs?"

Sam answered, "Sorry, dude, court order says you wear cuffs to the park, and you speak in front of the ghetto kids in cuffs and in orange."

Outside, they hopped into Sam's BMW, and off they went to the park.

⚾ ⚾ ⚾

Peter, looking at the Father, asked, "Father, is all that necessary?"

The response was quick and sure. "Pete, he hurt my kids. I said I was going to reach millions with him. But he does have a price to pay for his actions."

⚾ ⚾ ⚾

Eli reached inside of his Caddy, pulled out the key, and unlocked the cuffs. He then pulled out the sweats from a duffle bag and told Jamaal to get dressed.

When Jamaal came out of the locker room, he looked across the field for a place to run. Sam saw what he was doing and simply said, "Jamaal, go for it, man, and the rest of your life is lived in prison."

Jamaal realized that would be a huge mistake. Instead, he grabbed a glove.

His first throw was weak. Jamaal looked foolish with the endeavor. Eli shook his head.

"Jamaal, how do you expect to play ball like that?" Eli walked over and showed him how to throw it.

Jamaal threw a couple and began to get a feel for it. Eli could see just from his first couple of throws that this guy was a natural.

Next was batting practice. Aaron took Jamaal aside, showed him the swing, and said, "Have at it."

Jamaal got a sly grin on his face. "Hey Eli, you were a real hot shot pitcher. Let me see if I can hit your pitches."

Eli got a smile on his face and thought to himself, *this should be good.* He put his glove on and walked to the mound. He then threw a couple of pitches to the catcher to warm up.

He felt the juices start to flow. Eli could hear the music once again. He smiled and tossed the ball up in the air. He looked in at his catcher. He threw a couple more to make sure his arm was warmed up.

⚾ ⚾ ⚾

Pete looked to The Father. "Should he be doing this?"

The answer was quick. "Pete, Jamaal needs to see that Eli is the best pitcher ever, and still is. A couple of pitches will not hurt him."

⚾ ⚾ ⚾

Jamaal came to the plate. Eli looked down at him. The catcher realized that he was about to catch a pitch that was the fastest he would ever catch.

Eli tossed the ball up in the air a couple of times, then took his stance, and blew by Jamaal with a pitch at about 100 mph.

The look on Jamaal's face was priceless. The disbelief of what just blew by him was evident. The catcher had to pull his glove off because of the pain he felt.

Jamaal looked at Eli and said, "C'mon, one more."

Eli got a big grin on his face as he decided to throw the change up as Jamaal was ready for a fast ball.

Eli let it go. Jamaal swung two seconds early.

"C'mon, man, that's not fair!" Jamaal answered as he walked up to Eli.

"Jamaal, there is nothing fair in this life. Was it fair that you sold the kid meth? Get used to it, man. Just know this, when we tell you something, it's because we know what we are talking about."

Eli then slowed down his pitches so Jamaal could get a feel of what hitting a ball really felt like. The potential greatness that was Jamaal's was astounding. The thought in the back of Eli's mind was, *Where could this guy have gone if he had not messed up?*

Then the thought continued, *What about the rest of the kids in the ghetto? Can we somehow get them to realize that they have to work hard and that work will be rewarded?*

It's at this point Thumbnail whispered into Jamaal's ear for the first time. "Tell Eli that he should build a construction company in the ghetto, be a silent partner, and to hire a black man to run it."

Jamaal shrugged and asked, "Where did that come from?"

"I have an idea. The drugs are running rampant in the ghetto. Watts is being overrun by them. My uncle, Mike, has always wanted to start a construction company but has never been able to raise the capital. Wondering if maybe you would consider talking to him about a joint venture? If we could put the folks to work in Watts, then we may be able to do some good," Jamaal said to Eli.

"If we could put the folks to work in Watts, then we may be able to do some good?" he repeated.

Eli could hardly believe what he was hearing. The thought just went through his mind, and Jamaal was talking about it.

"Jamaal, I want you taking batting practice now! That is an interesting idea. We'll talk about it later," Eli answered quickly.

Eli looked over the field, saw some great defensive play, and said to Aaron and Sam, "Boys, I think we may just have us a baseball team here."

After practice, they had Jamaal shower and put his jumpsuit back on. For the ride back to the jail, Jamaal would also need to be cuffed.

On the way back, Eli told Jamaal, "I am gonna talk to Jill when I get home. We will pray about the construction company and go from there."

Jamaal got a strange look on his face and said, "You white boys always ask your women for permission before you do something. Don't you know that a real man just controls everything?"

The anger in Eli's voice was very noticeable. "Listen, Dude! That lady is the love of my life! She is not a piece of property! She is the one gift that Father has given me that is cherished above all else! Don't you ever speak of women in that tone with me again! Understood?"

Jamaal was quiet for the rest of the trip back to jail.

Arriving at home, Eli walked in, gave Jill a kiss and a hug, and felt Hannah kick in the womb. Eli smiled as he looked at his beautiful bride and said, "You're glowing, sweetheart. I am so proud to be your husband."

Jill cooed back, "You're going to be a great dad, sweetheart. I think of all those kids without a dad, and my heart cries out for them."

Eli could feel the Spirit speaking to him. "Hun, Jamaal came up with a great idea today, about the same time The Father was speaking to my spirit about it."

Jill answers quizzically, "What was that?"

"Well, Jamaal suggested I speak to his uncle in the ghetto. He said he has always wanted to start a construction company. I have been feeling like, if we can do something to help these kids make an honest living, then we won't have to deal with them selling drugs. On the ride back to jail, I got his uncle's name and number. I told him I would talk to you about it and that we would take it to prayer and see what Father had to say." Eli said, purposefully leaving out what Jamaal had said about women in general.

Jill raised one question. "What do you know about construction?"

Eli shook his head, "Not a thing, babes, not a thing. But Father constructed everything. I would be a silent partner."

Eli and Jill held hands and spent the next forty-five minutes in prayer, seeking their Father's face on the construction company. They were given names and numbers of contacts that would prove valuable in the venture.

After praying, Eli called Jamaal's uncle. "Hello, is this Michael Howard?"

Michael answered quickly, "It is."

"Mr. Howard, my name is Eli McBrien."

"The baseball player?" Howard asked Eli.

Eli gave a cocky answer, "The one and only!"

Michael gave a quick comeback, "You are the greatest pitcher ever! Why did you leave the game?"

"That, my friend, is an interesting question. I developed arthritis in my shoulder. Doc said if I quit, I could live a pretty normal life. If not, I would suffer forever. There are a lot of things I could do besides play baseball, like build a construction company right there in Watts. Give the folks there some hope. Mr. Howard, I want to make you president and be a silent partner. Interested?"

The answer came in the form of a question. "Mr. McBrien, that would take at least twenty million dollars just to buy the equipment, and we have no trained labor in the ghetto. How do you suppose we do this? I do not have that kind of money."

Eli responded with his own question. "Mr. Howard, what is your background, and can you tell me you could turn a profit here?"

With that, pride welled up in Michael Howard, "I am a graduate of the California School of Construction. I am presently the chief construction officer for the state of California. I just could never raise enough capital to start a company."

Eli nodded and said, "Well, let's meet for lunch next week. We have a game Wednesday and Thursday. Then I am taking my bride for a trip before our baby comes."

Michael said, "That leaves us Monday. Would that work for you?"

"Michael that would be great! Noon, at La Cochina's in the Sigma Mall?" Eli answered.

"That would be great," he answered quickly.

O O O

The Father looked over at Pete. "The new hospital they build would be just what Watts needs to turn that slum around."

Pete got a surprised look on his face. "A hospital?"

"That's right, Pete. Remember, Eli will be the silent partner, and ownership will be part of Michael's compensation for years to come."

"You see, I pour money into people who are going to advance my kingdom."

"I build ministries, and I tear them down when the people I put in them take their eyes off of me."

Pete got an "aha" look on his face. "Father, I remember a few."

O O O

Monday came. Eli and Michael met at La Cochina's for lunch.

Eli ordered the trout with lemon. Michael looked at the menu.

"Man, this is expensive!"

Eli answered, "Don't worry, I got it."

Michael ordered the same as Eli.

Eli started the conversation. "Michael, I want to do something in Watts that will start getting these young men into constructive occupations. We will do that by using two million as a downstroke, the balance from an SBA loan.

Sam Boursa and his cousin, Aaron, and I have started a baseball team. At the same time, we became parole officers for Jamaal."

Michael got an acknowledging look on his face. "Yah, I have heard all about that. You guys are making a ten-year commitment on this. But how would that get you to want to start a construction company?"

Eli answered, "It's like this. If we put these kids to work, and work 'em hard, then they will be too tired to mess people up."

"Maybe we could start to have a negative effect on the gang activity."

Eli ran his hand through his hair as he asked the question, "How much money are we going to need to get this whole thing started?"

Michael's quick answer was another question, "How big do you want to be?"

Eli gave a little chuckle, "Tell ya what, when I get back from our vacation, I will have an answer for you."

Just then, Eli's alarm went off on his phone. He had to get over to the jail to pick up Jamaal for practice.

Eli drove over to the jail. Jamaal was waiting for him in the visiting room, dressed in his prison orange, and wearing cuffs. Eli walked in.

"Sorry, man, I was running late." At that second, Eli's phone rang. Eli looked at the screen on his cell, it was Jill.

Eli answered the phone to a very hysterical wife. "Eli, I'm bleeding! I think I am in trouble!"

"I'm calling an ambulance. I will be there in a flash!" Eli looked at Jamaal and said, "Sorry, man, gotta run."

Eli was driving 115 mph on the freeway, weaving in and out of traffic. The lights went on behind him. "Lord, please help me!" he prayed.

Eli pulled over. The highway patrol woman came to the car. Eli opened his passenger side window so he could talk to the officer. Eli had his license and title when she got there.

"Officer, I just got a call from my bride. She is having a miscarriage, and I was trying to get there as quickly as I could. We have an ambulance on the way, and I need to get there!" Eli said in a panicked voice.

The young highway patrol woman looked at Eli. "Mr. McBrien, I lost one myself. Follow me, stay close. Tell me the address and I'll get you there."

Eli had no idea that his Caddy was as fast as it was. They were cruising on the freeway at 140 mph. They arrived at the condo in six minutes.

As they arrived, they were loading Jill into the ambulance, and Eli was going to follow them to the hospital.

They arrive at the hospital in another nine minutes, rushed Jill in, but it was too late.

The doctor came out, looked at Eli, and told him, "Jill is going to be okay, but they could not save your little girl."

Eli went into Jill's room. Jill sat up in the bed. Eli held her for what felt like hours. Jill sobbed in his arms.

Eli just kept saying "I love you, I love you, and I love you!"

6
The Red Hot Pitcher

I<small>T WAS</small> S<small>ATURDAY</small> morning. Eli woke in the chair beside Jill's bed. He thought to himself, *Has all of my concern for the scum of the earth contributed to my baby dying?*

He walked over and kissed Jill on the forehead. She woke, eyes still a bit teary, smiled, and said, "Eli, I love you. What are you thinking?"

"Just that, if I had been there, this might not have happened," Eli sobbed.

Dr. Jameson walked in. "Mr. and Mrs. McBrien, we did an extensive exam on the little girl. She had a severe heart abnormality. There was nothing anyone could have done. I do know your pain is intense, but I hope that brings some comfort to you folks."

Eli looked at the doctor, "If it had been caught, is there anything that could have been done?"

"No, Eli. It's just one of those things."

Peter looked at the Father and asked him the question that every person who suffers loss of this magnitude asks, "Father, why?"

The Father looked at Peter, with tears in his eyes. "Pete, I have their little girl right here with me. Peter, my Word does not say everything that happens is good. It says, all things work together for good to those who love me and are called according to my purpose. This is not a good thing that happened in their life, but I will work something good out of it. Watch, just watch."

Jill looked at Eli, "Hun, can we try again?"

Eli smiled with his big grin. "Of course we will try again. But this time, I will be a doting husband."

Jill looked at Eli. "Mister, this was hard, but you have other children as well. Our Father has given you a caring spirit for all these kids. Remember your secret ambition. I know our Father has children for us, like ten, at least. This will take some time, but our Father will get us through this."

Eli got a look of desperation on his face as he said one word, "Ten?"

Jill smiled.

There was a knock at the door. Sam and Aaron walked in.

They were trying to figure out just what to say. They both looked like two lost sheep as they shuffled around the room.

Jill piped up. "Okay, you two, we lost a baby, that's hard; but Father is in control. We are both hurting right now, and you're not helping by moping around."

Jill got a sly grin on her face. "I have an idea. There's a Dairy Queen within minutes from here. Blizzards are on sale. Buy the first at full price, and the second is a quarter."

Sam and Aaron got kind of a dumb look on their face like, "What are you talking about?"

Eli shook his head. "All right, guys, she gets out in the morning. Take the hint and go buy four blizzards. I like chocolate chip cookie dough myself."

Jill piped up with, "Reese's pieces here!"

The two Boursas simply said, "Okay. We'll be back in ten." With that, they were gone.

Jill looked at Eli, "Now here is the scoop. You need to talk to them when they get back about the game. Find out how Jamaal did. This is hard on both of us, but the distraction of working with Jamaal will be what gets you through this."

Eli got a concerned look on his face. "But what about you, babes? What will get you through it?" He then asked the question again. "If you send me off to work with the players, how do you get through it?"

Jill smiled. "You will be my distraction. I do have to keep you out of trouble, and I am setting up some grief counseling as well. Hun, this cut deep, but Christ will get us through it."

Eli's cell phone went off. It was Corrine. "Eli, are you with Jill right now?"

Eli answered emphatically, "Where else would I be?"

In her sweetest voice, Corrine responded, "May I speak to her?"

Eli looked at his sweetheart lying on the hospital bed. "It's Corrine."

"Hi, Corrine!"

"Jill!"

"Don't say a word, just get over here and give me a hug. This hurts, but we have to realize that Father is in control, and he really does know what is best in every situation," Jill said.

"Be there in a few. Love ya!" Corrine responded.

Jill handed the phone back to Eli.

Sam and Aaron returned with the Blizzards. "Tom Lipinski, the owner of Dairy Queen, sends his best. He says these are on the house."

Jill smiled. "That is so sweet of him." Jill got a stern look on her face. "The doctor is releasing me in a little bit. Corrine is going to the house with me. Eli, you need to get over to the jail and talk to Jamaal. Let him know what happened. Just make sure I get to the car, and Corrine can drive me home. But first, we have to set up some meetings with the grief counselor here."

Eli escorted his beautiful bride to the counselor's office. Walking into the office, Jill was greeted with hugs and warm hellos.

They walked into the office of Ben Wolfe, the foremost man for helping people through situations such as this. He looked at Jill and Eli. "I know you two have lost a child, yet everyone grieves in a different way. I think it would be better if we set up sessions for you two as a couple and individually."

"I just had someone cancel. I have some time now. Let's talk."

"Eli, can I use your cell phone for a second? I have to call Corrine."

She spoke with Corrine briefly then Jill hung up and said, "Corrine is taking me shopping this afternoon."

Ben looked at Jill and simply asked her, "What are you feeling right now?"

The quick anger that exploded about blew Eli away. Ben was not surprised at all.

"I'm mad at God and Eli and even myself for not taking better care of me and the baby! The doctor said there was nothing that could be done. How am I supposed to really know that?" Jill screamed at the top of her lungs.

Eli was about to say something, and Ben held up his hand as if to say, "Let her talk, she needs to vent this stuff."

Jill walked around the room, screaming and shaking her fist at God. She swore at Eli, making him feel like crawling under the table. Then exhausted, she fell into Eli's arms sobbing.

She then looked up at Eli, "I really, really do love you!"

Eli just held her. "I love you too, my most precious gift. I love you too!"

The Father looked at Peter, "All things work together for the good to those who love me and are called according to my purpose. I will use this hard part of their life to draw them closer together."

Peter nodded, realizing how Father's love really worked. "So you're going to have the pain that they are experiencing now and build them up to help others later?"

"That's exactly right, Pete. Even in one of my servants' pain, there is victory."

* * *

Eli stood, walked over to Jill, took her in his arms, and held her tight.

She pushed him away, "Don't touch me, just don't touch me!"

Eli put his hands on her shoulders, lowered his eyes to her level. "Babes, I will always love you, and we will get through this," he said.

Jill said in a quiet voice, "Hold me a little while, just a little while."

Ben looked at them and smiled to himself. *These kids will do okay*, he said to himself.

Jill, with her head still buried in Eli's shoulder, sobbed. "Take me home, hun. Just take me home."

The drive home was a quiet one. Eli was simply holding Jill's hand. He looked over at her, and she smiled. Eli melted in his seat. That smile still melted his heart.

Arriving back at the condo, Sam and Aaron were there, waiting.

Aaron spoke up, "We brought you Blizzards."

Jill chuckled a bit. She looked at hers, and it was milk. "Thanks, you guys, you're so sweet."

Walking into the house, Jill looked over at Eli, "Hun, could you stay with me tonight? We can get back to a normal life tomorrow." Then it struck her. "I've got to call Corrine. I was supposed to go shopping with her. Eli, give me your phone please."

Eli smiled, handed Jill his phone, and said, "Sure, hun." With that, Eli showed Sam and Aaron to the door. "Guys, let Jamaal know that I will see him tomorrow. Set up practice for tomorrow afternoon, okay?"

Eli then walked back to his beautiful bride. He touched her hair, took her hand, and simply sat down beside her. They sat in silence for a full hour, just looking into each other's eyes. They cried, they hugged, but not a word was said. As Eli looked deep into her eyes, he realized that Father had done something tremendous. He realized that the loss of Hannah would have some eternal benefit. He did not understand those thoughts at all. But a peace that he could not at this time understand came over him. It was the same peace he felt on the mound when his mother's friend prayed for him when he was pitching his last game before his surgery.

He looked over to Jill and simply said, "Sweetheart, Father is doing something. I don't know what, but He is doing something."

Jill looked back, and with a tear in her eye, simply said, "I know."

They spent the rest of the day praying and holding each other. The peace that came over them was truly the peace that surpasses all understanding.

Father looked over at Peter, "Do you realize what I was able to do here?"

Peter shook his head.

"Peter, I touched them with my Spirit. I brought them a peace that the world had no idea it had access to. I am going to give them assurance for the rest of their life on earth that Hannah will be waiting for them when they walk into my heaven. Peter, I see the beginning from the end. I am the Alpha and the Omega. I change lives, I touch hearts, and I make all things new."

Eli walked to the kitchen and prepared Jill a cup of hot chocolate with whipped cream and caramel on it. He handed it to her and simply smiled.

Jill, in her cute way, smiled back at him. "Sweetheart, you know how to make my heart sing. You really do. You are such a gift from our Father to me and to the children we will have." Then she got a quizzical look on her face. "Eli, I was just wondering. Do you think little Hannah will know us when we walk through the gates of our Father's heaven?"

Eli got a huge smile on his face. "I don't have a doubt in my mind."

Jill smiled as she said, "I sure do love you."

The next day, at two o'clock the next afternoon, Eli drove up to the jail, walked in, and Jamaal came out cuffed and in his jumpsuit. "Eli, I sure am sorry, man. I had no idea the pain you and Jill must be in. You really do love her a lot, don't you?"

Eli smiled, "Yeah, I really do. When Father gives you a gift, you gotta treasure it, man."

Eli walked around to open the door for Jamaal. Jamaal asked, "Will there be a time when

I don't have to wear cuffs to practice and the games?"

Eli gave a quiet chuckle, "Yeah, in a little under ten years." Jamaal shook his head.

When they got to the practice field, the rest of the team was warming up already. Their young pitcher was Samuel Adams. He had great speed, but control was an issue.

Eli walked over to him. "Listen, Samuel, it's no good to be able to throw a super fast pitch if you send the guy to base on balls. Let me show you some things."

The anger in Adam's voice caught Eli off guard. "Listen, I don't need you to show me anything. The only reason I am here is to prove to my b…that I can play baseball."

Eli shook his head. In a low almost-whisper voice, Eli said, "Listen, I am going to tell you this once, you have a choice: you play by my rules, or you will not play. I am not going to fool around with you." Eli stepped back, folded his arms across his chest, and waited for an answer. Samuel just stared at Eli, threw his glove down, picked it up, and stormed off the field.

Eli looked around and shouted, "Who thinks they can pitch and are willing to be taught?"

Up goes the hand of a skinny kid, Thaddeus Jones. "Mr. McBrien, could I try?"

Eli gave a little chuckle. "Sure, why not?"

⚾ ⚾ ⚾

The Father said to Pete. "Remember what I did with David and Goliath?"

Peter's excitement was showing as he said, "Father, is the little Thaddeus going to show some big stuff here?"

"Just watch. He has some hidden talent that Eli is about to uncover," Father stated with total confidence.

⚾ ⚾ ⚾

Eli thought to himself, *I think I am going to have Jamaal hit this kid. This will show him that pitching is really not his thing.*

Eli points to Jamaal. "Jamaal, get in the batter's box!"

Jamaal got up to the plate. Thaddeus got set and threw a curve ball that looked as if it is going to cross the plate. Jamaal wound up and swung. The ball looked like it swung out around the tip of the bat.

Jamaal's eyes about popped out of his head. "How did he do that?"

Eli just smiled.

The second pitch looked to be flying toward the plate, and just before it got there, it dropped like a rock. Jamaal was caught swinging again.

The third pitch was one that Eli had never mastered, the knuckle ball. It looked like it was floating and no spin on it at all. Jamaal swung, and the ball was an easy pop up.

Eli walked up to Thaddeus. "Where did you learn to pitch like that? I have not seen that level of pitching with some major league pitchers."

Thaddeus just smiled.

Father said to Pete, "What did I tell you? David and Goliath, David killed the giant. Young Thaddeus is going to be a giant killer, just watch."

Thumbnail, sitting on Jamaal's shoulder, told him, "Look, mister, you have got to concentrate on the ball more. Baseball is like life. You have got to wait on your pitches and see where they are going before you swing at them. You're making your decisions way too quick. It keeps get ting you in trouble. Look what not thinking about your choices has gotten you into. Just wait for the pitch to be where it needs to be before you swing."

Jamaal looked around himself. "Who said that?" He waved to Eli. "Can we try that again?"

Eli nodded and looked over at Thaddeus. "Give him some more pitches."

Thaddeus threw him a curve ball.

Thumbnail told him wait on this one. Jamaal waited to see if it started to spin, and let it go. "Ball one!" Eli hollered. "Good eye!"

Thad decided to see if he could hit his knuckle ball. Jamaal waited on it, saw it cross the plate, and slammed it for about four hundred feet. It was a fair ball and a home run.

Thumbnail whispered to Jamaal, "Wait on the pitches of life, you'll win every time."

After practice, Jamaal went to the locker room to change, came out in his orange prison jumpsuit, let Eli put the cuffs on him, and got into the Caddy.

On the way back, Jamaal said to Eli, "Man, it's like I had someone sitting on my shoulder. He was telling me that baseball is like life. I have to wait on my pitches. Just like before I make choices in life, I have to think out what the results will be."

Eli responded, "You're starting to get it, my friend. Sometimes, what seems like a home run pitch is a curve ball, or a sinker that you can't hit. You swing, you lose."

Jamaal smiled as he said, "You know, Eli, this baseball stuff, I think it's really a Godsend. I know that ten years will go by quickly."

Jamaal walked into the jail. He started getting razzed by the guys waiting trial there.

"Hey man, how do you rate such special treatment?"

Jamaal looked at the other person making the comments. "How long you in this place for?" was Jamaal's quick response.

"Ninety days" was the answer he got quickly.

Thumbnail took that instance to open conversation with the other inmate. "Tell him about God's grace in this whole thing," he told Jamaal.

Jamaal proceeded to go into detail about how he messed up little kids with meth. He went on to tell him about the cops busting his stash of meth. He shared that the sentence handed down to him was for 150 years, it was stayed for ten years in the county jail and probation for the rest of his life. The stipulation he agreed to was that he would be playing ball and telling the kids about how drugs will mess them up. The sentence also had him go to the games in cuffs and his jumpsuit then change there. He explained how he had met Eli, Sam, and Aaron and really blew a good situation. Then he explained how he quit running from Christ and allowed Him to take control of his life.

The other inmate simply shrugged and said, "Still not a bad deal for what you did man."

Anger started to well up in Jamaal. Thumbnail simply stated to him, "Hey dude, cool it."

⚾ ⚾ ⚾

St. Peter looked over at the Father and said, "Jamaal is not nearly as easy to get to as Eli was. His temper could get him in a lot of trouble.

Father chuckled a bit. "Pete, when are you going to learn to sit back and watch me work? But Thumbnail had to learn that the more experience he got, the harder the case I am going to send him on. You want to hear some interesting stories, then ask Gabriel about some of his experiences with Eli's mom's friend."

⚾ ⚾ ⚾

Eli walked into the condo, looked over at Jill, and ardently stated, "Hun, I really do love you."

She smiled back at him. "Did you have a hard day at practice?"

Eli got an exasperated look on his face as he said, "I just don't understand. I had a kid there, great fast ball, and he walked away because he did not want me to show him anything. I just don't get it."

A light went on inside Jill's head. "Could it be that he was feeling totally defeated, and he just needed some encouragement? Remember, you're not in Roseau anymore." The look she gave was of compassion for the young men that Eli had to work with. "These kids are coming from some of the toughest situations that a kid can be in. First, most have no dads, just a mom, or maybe not a good mom at that. Many times they have to scrounge for food and clothes…who knows." Jill continued.

Eli was quick to answer. "Then tell me, how should I have handled it? Just how do I reach that kid?"

Jill's education came into play here. "Eli, he challenged you, so challenge him back. If you tell him to strike out Sam over there, then he can do it his way. If Sam hits him, then he listens to your coaching."

Eli nodded his head, "Okay, I will call him tomorrow."

Jill shook her head in response and said with the voice of a mother, "Eli, you pick up that phone and call him now! You have his number in the registration form, don't you?"

"Okay, hun, you win. I will call him now."

Eli picked up the phone and called Sam. "Hello, is this Sam Adams?"

"You got me. What do you want?"

"This is Eli McBrien. We kind of got off on the wrong foot today. I am willing to let you pitch the way you want, on one condition. You pitch to Sam Boursa, you get him out and you pitch the way you want. You walk him or he gets a hit, you pitch my way; fair enough?"

Sam thought to himself, *There is no way that Boursa will get a hit from me. I am better than he is.* "You're on!" was Sam's answer.

The next day at practice, Eli was talking to Boursa about what his plan was.

He told Sam, "I want you to knock him out of the park if he can get the ball in. If he does not, then let him walk you."

It's Sam versus Sammy; Sammy walked out to the mound. Sam walked into the batter's box.

Sammy asked himself, *Why am I trying to pitch against thee Sam Boursa? Do I really think I am that good?*

Sammy looked at the catcher, signaled for a fast ball at the knees. Sammy threw one at about 102 mph, just about shoulder level. Boursa drove it out of the park."

Sammy said to Eli, "Okay, hot shot, show me how it is supposed to be done."

Eli just smiled and said, "Give me the ball."

Taking the mound, Sam looked at Eli and said to himself, *"I hate trying to hit this guy. Never could get him timed."*

Eli heard the music and looked to the catcher. The signal was for a fast ball at the knees. Eli just smiled and let a strike fly at about 101 mph.

Sam could not even get his bat around.

Eli threw a second fast ball. Sam swung just a bit late.

Eli followed that with his change-up, and Sam struck out.

Eli walked off the mound, tossed the ball into Sammy's glove, and said, "Ready to learn how to pitch?"

Sammy nodded, "You know it."

Eli yelled at Thaddeus, "C'mon, Thad, it's time to go to work."

Eli spent the next couple of hours working with the pitchers, getting them ready for the competition that would be starting the following week.

7
Jamaal's Real Freedom

IT WAS SATURDAY morning. Eli was attempting to sleep in. Jill was already up for the day when the phone rang. It was Eli's mom.

"Good morning, Jill. Hope all goes well. Could I speak with Eli?" Jill tried to be nice. "Eli is still sleeping. He had a really tough week with the team."

Grace was persistent. "Jill, this is really important! Please wake Eli up!"

Jill started to get irritated. "What can be so important that you want to wake my husband six in the morning?" Jill said very intensely.

Grace suddenly felt terrible, "Oops! I forgot the time difference. Would you have him call as soon as he gets up?"

Jill smiled to herself and thought, *Sometimes it pays to be tough for the one you love.* "Yes, Grace, I will have him call you as soon as he gets out of bed."

Two hours later, Eli dragged himself out of bed and came downstairs. Jill said to him, "Eli, your mom called. She asked you to call her as soon as you get out of bed."

Eli pulled out his cell and dialed his mom. "Hi, Mom, what's up?"

"Eli, just wanted to tell you about your little brother. He is pitching in little league. He is doing pretty well."

Eli responded, "Mom, that's great! I am glad you did not wake me up to tell me that, however." With that, Eli said good-bye to his mom. Eli looked over at Jill and said, "I have a great day planned. I will drink my coffee and then I am going to take you, my bride, out to breakfast."

Jill looked at Eli, "Really?"

"Let's go! Jerry's on the beach."

When they arrived, the water was like glass, and they were at a window seat overlooking the ocean.

As they were ordering breakfast, a little boy came to the table, smiled at Eli and Jill, and asked for Eli's autograph. "Why, sure, young man, and who do I make this out to?"

The boy answered, in somewhat of a weak voice, "My name is Tommy. You see, Mr. McBrien, I am not going to be here much longer. Could you make it out to my mom? I would like her to have something special to remember me by."

Eli looked at his mom, then at Jill. "Tommy, what's your mom's name?"

Tommy looked at his mom. "Janice."

Eli excused himself and walked to the other side of the restaurant where Janice was sitting. "Janice, what's wrong with Tommy?"

"Tommy has a rare form of leukemia. There is only one bone marrow transplant in a million that will work. He has O-negative blood."

Eli excused himself, walked over to his bride, and gave Jill a kiss on the cheek. "Hun, you have O-negative blood, don't you?" he asked.

Jill got a puzzled look on her face. "Yes, why?"

"Go talk to Tommy's mom for a moment," he asked ever so sweetly.

"Pete, do you see how in this instance, all things will work for the Good, and does this help you understand divine appointments?" Then the Father continued. This may help you understand why I do what I do."

Pete answered, "Yes, Father, I think I do."

Jill walked over to Janice, "What is wrong with Tommy?"

Janice had tears running down her cheek as she told Jill what the problem was.

Jill looked at Janice and started crying. "I had a miscarriage last month. We lost a little girl. Why don't I get checked? If my marrow is a match, then we can use it."

All Janice could say was, "Thank you!" Not holding much hope that it would work.

Before Jill and Eli were able to arrive back at their condo, Jill's phone rang. "This is Jill. Yes…aha…we'll be there, two o'clock. That will be fine."

Eli, with a very questioning look on his face, asked, "What was that about?"

"I have an appointment to check my bone marrow, to see if I am a match for Tommy," was the sweet answer his beautiful bride gave.

🌕 🌕 🌕

Pete looked to Father. "Father, am I seeing another miracle here?"

The Father chuckled. "Pete, there are no miracles with me. This is what I do every day."

🌕 🌕 🌕

At 2:00 p.m. sharp, Jill and Eli arrived at the clinic for the test. Eli walked in with Jill, and they sat down and waited. The receptionist came out and said, "Jill McBrien." Eli started to get up to go with her. "Sorry, Mr. McBrien, but you must sit here," the nurse told Eli in a very stern voice.

Eli simply shrugged and sat back down.

Jill went into the examining room. She was told to lie on her stomach. They inserted a needle into her. There was some pain, but not a great deal. After a small sample of marrow was pulled, she was told she could get up and leave. The nurse told her she would be notified if there was a match. She was also told not to get her hopes up, as the boy was a very, very rare case.

Two weeks went by, and Eli had his first game as a coach. His team won big time. Jamaal got two home runs, and both Sammy and Thaddeus got their first wins.

Jill was shopping with Corrine when her cell went off. "Hi, this is Jill."

The nurse on the other end responded, "Jill, this is Helen Johnson from Park Hill Clinic. You're a match. Are you still willing to donate?"

"Yes, of course! When?" was Jill's immediate response.

"Tomorrow at six in the morning. Can you check in tonight?"

"Of course!"

Jill hung up and called Eli. "Hun, I am a match! I AM A MATCH!"

The answer from Eli was quick. "Sweetheart, when do you donate?"

His greatest gift answered ever so sweetly. "I have to check in tonight, and they pull the marrow in the morning. I go home the same day."

That night Eli took his beautiful bride to a great restaurant then to the hospital.

As Jill slept, Eli walked the hall. He walked past little Tommy's room. His mom was beside the bed. Eli could tell that she was hurting. Eli stepped into the room ever so quietly. He put his hand on Tommy's mom's shoulder and simply asked if he could pray for her.

She smiled at Eli through her tears and simply said, "Please do."

Eli simply prayed. "Father, I know you have this under control. Give Janice the peace that passes understanding. Give little Tommy many more years to serve you. I ask these things in Jesus's name." He smiled, touched her shoulder, and left the room and walked to Jill's.

Eli slept in the chair beside Jill's bed. He wanted to be there to take Jill home in the morning after the procedure.

Morning came quickly. The nurse came in, and they pushed Eli out of the way so they could get Jill to the procedure room. The whole process would be a huge success. Tommy would live to be a huge success. His legend would be so great stories would be written about him for many years to come. He would play college ball at Nebraska and fifteen years as a pro with Minnesota. But it would be his music that he would be remembered for the most. He would be a huge factor in teaching young kids the value of never ever giving up.

The next day, Eli and Jill had breakfast. Eli looked at his bride, kissed her forehead ever so gently, and walked off to go to pick Jamaal up at the county jail.

Eli walked back to meet with Jamaal. "Hey, bud, your hittin' keeps getting better and better." Then he continued, "I hear you have a meeting with the First Church to get their anti-drug program going?"

"That's right. I'm supposed to go in this ugly orange jumpsuit again," Jamaal complained.

Eli smiled to himself. "Yup, you gotta play by the rules. Those kids gotta see what happens when you mess with the Man," Eli said as he pointed up.

Jamaal just shook his head.

Thumbnail jumped up and down on Jamaal's shoulder, knowing that this was the best for him as he said, "Listen to me and hear me! What you're going to tell these kids is exactly what you did. Oh yeah, you know that first little kid you gave the stuff to? He's dead."

Jamaal shook his head, "Who said that? I know he's dead. I watched him die." Then he looked around behind the door, even under his bunk. "Who said that?" he asked.

Jamaal walked out, hanging his head. The pastor was at the jail to meet him. The pastor had been made aware of the pain and trouble Jamaal had caused. The pastor had even met with the little red-headed boy's mom understood that she was still in very deep pain and extremely angry. She felt that the sentence Jamaal received was totally unjust. Her little innocent boy had been killed by this man and had gotten off with ten years in the county jail.

Pastor Johnson asked Jamaal, "Do you realize how much damage you have done to some of these kids? Jamaal, at some point, I want you to meet with the little red-headed boy's mom. I think it would be good for her to vent and meet face-to-face with her son's killer."

Jamaal hung his head as he answered the question, "Yes, sir, I do. I think God sent me a clear message and showed me just how much damage I have done. And to meet his mom is not something I really want to do."

The pastor asked, "What do you mean? Are you too much of a coward to meet the mom of the boy you killed?"

"I was in my cell a few minutes ago. I heard this voice, clear as a bell. It told me that one of the children, the first one I gave this crap to, died. It really shook me up! I don't understand why it shook me up so much now when it did not back then. I watched him die. I knew he was dead. It just hit me like a ton of bricks. And yes, I am too much of a coward to meet his mom. I do know that it is something I really need to do though."

He got up, started to walk across the room, picked up a chair, and threw it. He started yelling, "Why did I do that crap? Why?"

🔘 🔘 🔘

Thumbnail smiled.

The Father said to Pete, "The truth gets them every time."

🔘 🔘 🔘

Jamaal was crying as he paced the room. Pastor Johnson sat and watched; he just watched. He knew what the prompting to say something felt like, and it was not there. He just let Jamaal vent his anger at himself. He walked over, and Jamaal fell into his arms. "Can God forgive me for hurting his kids?" Jamaal said between sobs.

"Just ask him," the pastor responded.

Jamaal prayed with the two pastors that were there to meet with him. True remorse was flowing through Jamaal. He stated, "I really do deserve 150 years. By the grace of God, I am in this situation now. Let's reach these kids."

Pastor Johnson said to Jamaal, "Our first meeting is next Wednesday afternoon. I believe you have a night game, so we are bringing the kids out to see you. Jamaal, you have done great damage. Now the Lord is giving you a chance to do good."

Jamaal looked at Pastor Johnson and said, "You and I know that there is no forgiveness for what I have done, so why even bother? I can do all the good in the world, why would God forgive me? I killed one of his kids."

Johnson looked at Jamaal. "Who told you that?"

"God did," was the quick answer from Jamaal.

Johnson looked at Jamaal. "That, my son, was not God you were listening to. What you did to that boy, my son, is something you have to live with. But know this, Christ died so that we could have newness of life. He does use all things for His good for those who love Him and who are called according to *His* purpose. Let's let God touch the hearts of countless kids through your life."

Jamaal nodded. "I better get working on just what I'm going to say. Be praying for me, please?"

Thumbnail took the opportunity to speak loudly, "Don't worry, dude, I will tell you exactly what the Father wants."

Jamaal looked around, trying to figure out who was talking to him. Again, he even looked under the chair he was sitting on.

Johnson was laughing, "What are you looking for man?"

"Someone just told me that God would tell me exactly what to say. Actually, the term was *The Father*."

"Really?" was the only response Johnson could come up with.

The Father looked over at Pete. "Pete, you have been with me now for a couple of thousand years. You have seen me work in people's lives. How do you think I am going to work with Jamaal?"

"Father, I have seen you work with millions of people. The amazing thing is, you can work with so many at one time and yet be personal with each one. I do know that each person is different. You have made all of us unique. I have no idea what you're going to do."

"Pete, stand back and watch me work!"

◉ ◉ ◉

The next day at practice, Jamaal was just kind of going through the motions. Sam looked over at him and yelled, "Jamaal, get your butt in gear! Where is your hustle, man? I want to see some power in those hits at batting practice, and when you're in the field, you better hustle your butt! My patience is getting real short with you, dude!"

Thumbnail decided to join in the fun. "Jamaal, get it in gear. All those kids are going to be watching to see if you really are going to be a man about your punishment, or are you going to slough your way through the next ten years and mark time. The Father wants total commitment from you!"

Jamaal looked around again. "Am I going nuts? Who is telling me these things?"

Then Jamaal heard Thumbnail giggling. Jamaal, shaking his head, tried to figure out exactly who was talking to him.

Just then, Thumbnail heard Father's voice. "Thumbnail!"

"Gotcha, Father," was Thumbnail's response as the little angel turned red with embarrassment.

Practice being over, Eli was driving Jamaal back to his jail cell.

"Eli, do you have an extra Bible?" Jamaal asked.

"Yeah, lying on the back seat. Why do you ask?" Eli responded. Eli reached back, grabbed the Bible he had in the car, and gave it to Jamaal.

"Eli, the first time I saw you and you hopped up on the hood of your Challenger, you told us this was the source of real power. Did you mean that?"

Nodding, Eli responded, "It is the source of the real power. Nothing else even comes close. Did you know, that you can have God Almighty, through His Son by His Spirit, dwelling inside you all the time?" Eli asked.

"How do I do that?" was the answer that Eli wanted to hear.

"Simple, just stop running from Christ, repent, and believe. You will be saved."

Jamaal said, "How do I do that?"

Eli pulled the car over and put his hand on Jamaal's shoulder and said, "Pray, simply pray."

Jamaal's quick response was, "Can you help me with that?"

Eli put the Caddy in park. The two men joined hands and prayed, and Jamaal became a new part of the body of Christ.

As they pulled up to the jail, Eli said, "Jamaal, you have a new freedom in your life. You're free from those sins that put you here. You still have to pay the price, but that price is just here. God has thrown your sins into the sea of forgetfulness.

"Jamaal, remember this, you've been given new life in Christ. It's time to walk into that cell that is before you and glory in the fact that Christ has chosen to set you free from sin and death. If you had not changed, then your destiny would be death. Walk in the newness of life, and let your fellow inmates see it."

Eli escorted Jamaal in, said his good nights, and then he drove home. He was so excited he could hardly wait to see his beautiful bride and tell her all about Jamaal.

Eli walked in, saw Jill sitting quietly at the counter with soft Christian music playing in the background.

Jill looked up and smiled at Eli. "Something great happened today. I can see it in your face," Jill said, smiling.

"It really did! Jamaal accepted Christ! When I dropped him at the jail, he was flying."

Jill got a sly grin on her face as she said, "Hun, I think we should celebrate."

8
Deadly Truth

THE EARLY MORNING light sparkled off the ocean and shone into their bedroom. Rolling over on one arm, Eli puts his other arm around his bride and kissed her forehead as she slept. With his fingertips, he traced her eyebrows as she started to wake ever so gently. He said, "Your eyes are like the doors to heaven. They are so deep, yet so tender, and that which is behind them is as pure as the driven snow."

Jill opened her deep blue eyes, looked at her husband, and said, "Sweetheart, your mother raised a man after the Father's own heart, one who I trust with my very being. And, my dear, that trust started when you would not break that one promise my dad had you make."

"I could stay here beside you all day, every day. However, we both have a full day ahead of us. Oh, that promise. I have never had one that was so tough to keep. You don't know how many times I looked at your sweet lips and want to kiss them. Then I heard that one little voice, 'Wait, it will be worth it,'" Eli said as he kissed her ever so gently.

"What do you mean both of us?" Then came the question Eli was not ready to answer, but he knew he had to.

"Well...I kinda thought, maybe, you might want to get together with Corrine and lead a group of young ladies at the church to explore what it really means to be a woman of God," voiced the first sheepish answer Eli would give Jill.

Jill sat up in bed. Eli admired her greatly. And she quickly pulled the blanket up.

"Does Corrine know about this?" Jill asked in a perturbed voice.

Again, the sheepishness of Eli's answer was, "Not exactly. Well, by now she does. Sam was going to talk to her this morning."

"Okay, mister! Here's what's going to happen! I'm going to take a shower. You will call Sam and Corrine and invite them to breakfast. I am not opposed to the suggestion, but for a super stud pitcher, you sure tried the back door on this one. It better not ever happen again, or there will be words. And believe me, you have not ever seen me really angry, and you don't want to!"

Eli heard the water start running and called Sam.

"Sam, why don't you and Corrine come over for breakfast so we can talk about this?"

"I think that's good idea! Seems we have a couple of upset wives!"

"No kidding! But...," was Eli's quick response.

Twenty five minutes later, Sam and Corrine were ringing the doorbell.

Jill let them in and winked at Corrine.

As Sam walked into the next room out of earshot, Jill said to Corrine, "When should we tell them about praying about this very thing?"

Corrine responds mischievously, "Let's let them suffer a bit on this one. They have to learn not to try and manipulate us to do the will of our Father."

⚾ ⚾ ⚾

Pete looked to the Father and said, "Father, you have given both Eli and Sam very independent women."

Father responded quickly, "No, Pete, I have made two women who love truth. I am going to use them to teach Eli and Sam that if they aren't truthful, they will pay a price. Truth matters, and it will, from now on, always be honored in their marriages."

⚾ ⚾ ⚾

The four of them sat down to eat the blueberry pancakes that Eli had made.

Jill spoke up first. "You two can do some really dumb things sometimes! Why did you try to manipulate us? Why not just come straight out and tell us what was going on?"

⚾ ⚾ ⚾

The Father spoke again to Peter. "The most important thing a wife can do is to respect her husband. There is nothing a husband can do to wreck respect than to not be fully open with his wife. They have to learn that truth is paramount in any relationship."

Peter nodded.

◑ ◑ ◑

Corrine looked across the table and with an intensity that has not been seen by Sam before. "Look, you guys, Jill and I have been praying about this for months. For you two to try to get us to go into it without discussion is hurtful!"

Jill added, "We have seen the lack of respect that those young men have for the young ladies, and you two have shown us no respect here either. This better not ever happen again. The results will not be civil. We deserve truth, not manipulation."

Eli and Sam were both totally embarrassed about the whole thing. They both admitted just how wrong they were, agreed not to let it happen again, and to man up and be totally truthful about what was on their minds.

◑ ◑ ◑

The Father stated. "You see what happened here Pete. Eli and Sam were dealing with truth. I put it on all of their hearts to help the young ladies and thus the young men in the ghetto to start having relationships that honor me. The problem was they were planning on getting their help mates that I gave them to join them without being up front about my leading. That is using the truth in way that manipulates. It's always more honoring to just be upfront."

The next day the girls met with Pastor Johnson. They decided the best course of action to take. The one thing they didn't anticipate was the reaction of the young men from the ghetto would have with all of the young ladies suddenly demanding respect for themselves.

Jamaal's buddies came to see him in jail. Lionel told Jamaal, "You better get those Christian girls to stop coming in and getting our women all riled up about us respectin' them, or they will pay."

Thumbnail told Jamaal to warn them. "All right, you guys, listen up. Those women aren't "girls," they're women of God. If you try touching them, I don't know what my Father in heaven is going to do to you."

Later that day, Eli and Jill showed up at the jail to bring Jamaal to practice.

Ten minutes later, they arrived at the field. The gang members were there as well.

Eli was working with the pitchers. The girls were sitting on the bleachers.

Jamaal's "friends" decided to sit beside the girls. Sam saw them first and signaled to Eli. Both men walked up to the bleachers and started to walk toward the girls. Jill and Corrine looked somewhat frightened.

The biggest one started to grab Corrine's arm. She quickly grabbed his arm, swung it around his back, and dislocated his wrist in a judo move taught to her by her father, a former Navy Seal.

The baseball team spotted what was going on and surrounded the guys. Eli and Sam just stood back and let the team defend the girls.

Jamaal stated, "If you guys even think about coming against these ladies, you will be sorry you were born. Remember what Christ said when they brought Him the children? It would be better that a millstone was tied around your neck than you cause one of these little ones to stumble."

      ⚾ ⚾ ⚾

Then as they started to leave, God had Gabriel show up with one thousand angels with fiery swords. Gabriel said to the boys, "You want trouble, touch these women. You're not men, you're not even boys; you're less than animals for wanting to get Gods children to be used for your sick pleasure. If you're smart, you will listen to what Eli and Sam are trying to tell you. Don't mess with them, or we will destroy you."

The Father looked over at Peter. "Those boys won't go near my kids."

Peter responds, "What if they do?"

"They will regret the day that they were born," came the quick answer.

      ⚾ ⚾ ⚾

The boys didn't walk away, they ran in absolute terror.

Jamaal heard Thumbnail giggle. He started looking all over the place again, trying to see who was laughing.

He asked himself, "Why am I hearing that voice?"

Thumbnail heard Father's stern voice, "Thumbnail!"

Thumbnail just kept giggling.

Corrine said, "Looks like these little girls scared them, eh?"

Eli and Sam looked at each other and nodded and smiled.

"Okay, guys, let's get back to work!" Eli yelled.

The rest of the practice went as planned.

Arriving back at their condo, Eli looked at Jill, smiled, and said, "Babes, interesting day, eh?"

Jill got a questioning look on her face as she said, "Eli, you did not tell me that those brutes think so little of women. I am really relieved that Corrine learned so much self-defense from her father."

Eli got really interested at this point. "Uh, babes, how much did her daddy show her?"

Jill got that sly smile on her face. She walked up to Eli, placed her fingers on his Adam's apple. "She told me her dad has showed her how to pull the Adam's apple out of a man's throat and hand it back to him before he died."

"Does Sam know this? She is such a little thing. I would never have known she was so deadly."

Peter looked over at the Father. "Father, is she really able to do those things?"

"Peter", the Father said, "I have people learn things for a reason. There will come a time when she has to put one of those bullies on his back, and when she does, he won't get up, and he won't be here."

Peter looked surprised, even at him.

*   *   *

Just then, Eli's phone rang. "This is Eli. Hey Sam, what's up? Uh huh…yes…okay. I will pass it on to Jill. She wants to start the class next week. Gotcha!"

Eli took Jill by the hand, "Corrine wants to teach self-defense to the girls in the ghetto. She thinks it will help their self-esteem. I think she is right. She has talked to Pastor Johnson, and he agreed."

Jill responded, "I think that is great! I could use some of that training myself."

Eli shook his head, "I'll have to watch it around you. I really don't want to get hurt."

Jill laughed.

Three days later, they had their first meeting at the church with the young ladies.

They were starting their Bible study when the thugs from the ghetto came walking into the church.

The leader of the gang shouted, "These are my women. I own them. C'mon, girls, it's time to leave."

Corrine walked up to him, went nose-to-nose, and told him to leave.

He grabbed her by the neck. (Big mistake.) She forced his hand off of her neck and told him, "Listen, you thug, you have fifteen seconds to get out of here."

"And what if I don't?" the thug retorted.

"Then they will carry you out, and there is no guarantee you will be alive when they do," Corrine replied. She continued, "This is your warning. I have a third-degree black belt. Don't mess with me, I don't want to hurt you."

Once again, he grabbed her by the neck. She forced his hand away and drove a hard punch into his sternum, breaking it. His eyes got big; he tried to get a breath and dropped to the floor.

Corrine's face turned to a ghost-white shade as she looked down on the thug. Tears started to come to her eyes as she realized the power that she really did possess. She started to shake. The other women in the church quickly gathered around her for the support she needed desperately.

Then it hit her, she may have just sent this guy to... And the tears started to flow like rivers.

The gang got real quiet. They walked out one by one. Jill dialed 911. The police and ambulance crew came quickly.

They looked at the huge guy on the floor.

"Who did this?" one of the officers asked.

Corrine stood out. "That would be me, officer. I don't know if he is breathing or not."

The officer got a strange look on his face. "Tell me what happened."

Corrine went through the whole scenario of what happened. All the other girls concurred.

"Well, ma'am, I believe you, but you're going to have to come downtown and fill out a report."

Jill got on her phone and called Sam. "I think you may want to go to the police station and meet Corrine."

"Why is that?" was Sam's quick question.

Jill, fighting to hold back the tears, answered, "A guy came in and threatened the girls. To protect them, Corrine had to use her martial arts. It was not a pretty sight."

Sam sprinted out of the house and down to the car, forced himself to drive in a reasonable manner. He got to the station as they were already releasing Corrine.

Sam took her hand, looked into her eyes, and asked her, "Sweetheart, are you alright?"

Holding back tears, she said, "I am. He grabbed me by the neck. I told him not to do that. I just about broke his hand when I pulled it off my neck. Then he pulled his hand out of mine. I told him I was a third-degree black belt, and if he tried it again, I was afraid of what could happen to him." She whispered, "Sam, I am so sick...I had...I hope I never have to do that again."

Sam got a serious look on his face. "What happened then, Corrine?"

Corrine started to cry. "I pushed him away, and then he grabbed my neck again. I hit him in the sternum, really hard, and it drove the bone right into his heart." She finished with "I have been assured that no further action would be taken against me."

Sam held her close as she cried in his arms. They walked out, Sam holding Corrine close. As they walk out of the police headquarters, there were hundreds of women, of every color, standing outside, applauding her bravery.

Jamaal watched from the window of his jail cell. Thumbnail said to him, "Father always protects his kids." Again, Jamaal looked all over, trying to find out who was talking to him.

⚾ ⚾ ⚾

Eli and Jill ran up to Sam and Corrine. "Are you okay?" Eli asked.

"Yeah, I am okay. A bit scared, but okay," Corrine responded.

Jill answered, "It's time to go home. We need to regroup and see just how the Father wants us to handle this."

Sam looked at Eli, "Man, this has to stop! All this crap has to stop!"

Eli answered, "You know this, and I know this, but how do we accomplish it?"

Just then, Pastor Johnson drove up, hopped out of his car, and ran up to Corrine.

"Are you alright?"

Corrine then started to tell him the whole story. The young pastor looked at both Eli and Sam.

He said, "When these guys were raised, they either had no dad, or the one they had treated their mom like a cheap whore. It's a classic picture of a father's sin being passed from one generation to another. It has to be broken."

In unison, Sam and Eli said, "And how do we do that?"

The young pastor answered, "We start with prayer. That simple! It's not going to be an overnight fix. Jamaal is the key to the whole thing."

The Father looked over at Peter. "See, I told you! I have everything under control, but Thumbnail is driving Jamaal nuts," Father said with a smile in his eyes.

The Pastor and the two couples joined hands to pray.

As they were praying, a light went on inside Jill's head. "The key to the whole thing is Jamaal. Somehow, we have to reach him. Part of his sentence was to reach the kids and keep them off of drugs. What better way to do that than for them to learn to respect not only the other sex, but to respect themselves enough to realize that the Father's will is for them to be all that they can be. The only way they can do that is to have total respect for themselves and others."

Eli scratched his head. "My dear, tell me how that is going to be accomplished?"

Jill, shaking her head, put it simply, "Eli, respect either for self or for someone else has to be earned. Self-respect comes when a person actually works at something and accomplishes it. So let's say Jamaal is able to start working with the young kids to keep them off of drugs. He talks to them about the damage it does to them and then to others. He has to do this for ten years. He will see lots of kids come and go, but as he starts to see success and sees one generation build another, he will start to feel respect for himself in what he is doing."

Eli nodded as Corrine added, "We start with using his baseball prowess then build off of that. As the young boys start to look up to him because of his ability, and he builds his relationship with Christ, then his self-respect will start to build. When that happens, he will, hopefully, realize that Christ has created everyone with abilities that make them totally unique. And it is that uniqueness, that each one has, that makes each and every one of us worthy of respect as a child of the King."

Sam, with a look of astonishment on his face, said, "Ladies, you have got something here. I think we need to really find a way to get Jamaal doing a whole lot more than just serving a sentence. We need him to become an integral part of what Christ is doing here."

9

The Battle Is the Lord's

IT WAS SIX in the morning, and Jamaal was fast asleep in his cell. Thumbnail was sitting on the pillow beside his head. Father had been working, instructing Peter all night how he was going to speed up the process so as to get Jamaal up to speed with teaching the young ladies and men of the ghetto respect for each other now so it could be passed onto generations later.

The signal was sent, and Thumbnail started to sing into Jamaal's ear, "It's time to get up, it's time to get up, it's time to get up in the morning!"

Jamaal woke up, looked around, and said to himself, "Must have been dreaming." He rolled over and went back to sleep.

This time, Thumbnail was not quite so nice. He yelled, "I told you it's time to get your behind out of this bunk! You have to open the Bible now! There are things God wants you to read."

Jamaal rolled off of his bunk. He looked around his cell for his bible. Spotting it he walked across his cell and picked it up. Being dyslexic, he could not understand why the letters all looked right. He set the Bible down, walked across the cell, picked up a newspaper, and the words were, as usual, backward.

Thumbnail, sitting on his shoulder, simply said, "Jamaal, we will deal with the natural problem later. Our Father in heaven has just straightened the letters and gave you the ability to read His Word."

Luke, chapter 17, he read: "It would be better for a millstone to be tied around their neck than cause one of those little ones to stumble."

Thumbnail went on a rant, "Listen, Jamaal, Father does not have time for anyone who hurts His kids. His kids are little, and they're full-grown. Your friends don't respect anyone, not even themselves. When they take young women and treat them like cheap whores, then the young ladies start acting like it. Father hates that. It's time for you to start treating God's kids like the royalty that they are. The message of self-respect has to come out strong when you start talking to the young people about drugs this week."

Once again, Jamaal started looking all over his cell. *Who is talking to me?* he asked himself.

Thumbnail said to him, "Listen, it does not matter who is talking to you. Think about what has just been said to you."

Jamaal spent the next hour reading and rereading Luke. He looked up to heaven and said, "Father, I get it, I really get it. I now understand the dangers I was placing your kids in. I am so sorry. Help me to touch the kids for your purpose, not for the scum of the earth. In Jesus's name, Amen."

He ate breakfast at eight thirty. He took his Bible into the dining area. As he was eating, he was reading. He could not seem to put the Word down. He read 1 Corinthians 7:1: "It is good for a man not to touch a woman."

"Wow! So a dude should get married, wow! God really wants his kids protected. Wow!"

Two hours later, Eli showed up to pick up Jamaal to take him to the Civic Center to talk to the kids about drugs. Jamaal put on the cuffs and walked out to Eli's Caddy. They got in and drove to the Civic Center. Eli asked, "Do you have it worked out, what you're going to say to the kids?"

The answer and excitement that Jamaal gave caught Eli by surprise. "Yah, man! We are going to talk about respect today. About respecting yourself enough not to do drugs, and respecting others enough to tell them to stay away as well. It's about respecting each other and not taking advantage of them for our own gain. I am going to talk about Scripture, about fearing God, and about how much God really loves His kids. I am going to talk to them about really letting God be their Father, being the Father they may not have ever had. I am starting to feel like God is really my Father."

Eli smiled, almost in disbelief. He wondered to himself, *Where did he get this stuff?*

Thumbnail jumped over to Eli's shoulder and said, "It's all me, bro, it's all me."

The Father said sternly, "Thumbnail, who?"

"It's all you, Father."

"Better" was the response the Father gave back to Thumbnail.

Jamaal got a serious look on his face as he asked Eli, "Hey man, do you think God would be all right with me just calling him Father?"

Eli got a huge smile on his face. "Man, I think he would like that!"

Arriving at the Civic Center, Jamaal became very nervous. "What if my bros from the hood start trouble?"

Eli's answer was quick. "Don't worry about it. There will be police there to make sure that does not happen."

As they arrived, Eli walked to the podium. The place was packed. The worship band from Pastor Johnson's church had been playing.

Eli introduced Jamaal.

"My friends and bros, if you will. For too long I have been part of the hood. Being part of the hood, I thought the only way to get ahead was to do so by doing things that destroyed lives. I was wrong! When I read in God's Word 'that it would be better for a millstone to be tied around a neck than cause one of these little one to stumble,' I shook in my boots. I was causing God's little ones to stumble. The more I read it, it was almost like I was hearing one of God's messengers yelling in my ear."

Thumbnail said into Jamaal's ear, "Almost?"

○ ○ ○

Peter looked at the Father, "Should we put a few more controls on Thumbnail? He is getting a bit mouthy, is he not?"

The Father answered, "He gets excited and does not think sometimes, but I get a kick out of him. Remember, he serves Me. He says things in his excitement. But all he says, I use."

○ ○ ○

Jamaal continued, "Kids, it's no use. The only way you or I or anyone can see any meaning to our lives is to give our lives over to the one who created us for His glory and purpose. We need to be seeking His face every day so that when we make a decision, it is where He is leading us and not the enemy."

Just then a young lady spoke up. "Hey dude, you are the one who sold my ten-year-old nephew that crap. He is dead! How do you deal with that, you murderer?"

The young lady walked up to the podium and hands Jamaal a picture of her dead little nephew.

Jamaal started to sob uncontrollably.

Again the young lady spoke up. "Don't ever begin to tell me how sorry you are. There is nothing you can do to bring back my nephew. They should have let you rot in jail for the rest of your life! You took something that can't be replaced. He was only ten! Ten years old and you gave him the crap that killed him! I hope you burn in hell!"

Eli looked at Sam. "Now you know why I am still dealing with what he did. It stole the innocence of a kid, and it killed the kid in the process. And we got this guy off easy! I sure hope we are in God's will on this."

Jamaal looked at Eli and Sam. He was sobbing totally out of control.

"Why did God let me do what I did?"

Eli and Sam looked at him. Eli said, "He stopped you. You're lucky he did not kill you and send your soul to hell."

Jamaal said, "What do I do now?"

Eli answered, "Just what you're doing. It's not going to be easy, but you have to be able to reach kids for Christ and teach them to say no. Let's get you back to jail."

With that, they cuffed Jamaal, got him back in the Caddy, and took him back to jail.

The incident had angered Eli so much that he could not even look at Jamaal. He took him into the jail. They took the cuffs off of him, and Eli just walked away.

Peter looked over at the Father. "Father, redemption is not an easy thing sometimes, is it?"

The Father looked over at Christ, sitting on the throne of judgment, and said, "It cost my Son everything so Jamaal could be redeemed. His redemption is paid for. He does have to pay the price of hurting my kids. That price is paid on earth. I am breaking Jamaal, and he will no longer complain about spending time in jail."

◍ ◍ ◍

Jamaal walked into his cell. His cellmate looked at him. "Hey man, what's up? You look like you have been through the wringer."

Jamaal just started to cry again. "I deserve the chair. I deserve the most horrible death known to man, but God chose to save me. I destroyed someone precious to our Father in heaven, a child."

His cellmate looked the other way. "Look, dude, that's something you gotta live with. You have your sentence. Serve your time and get on with it."

Jamaal shook his head and shouted. "It has to stop, it just has to stop!"

◍ ◍ ◍

Eli arrived back at the condo, walked inside, and threw his back against the wall.

"Why, why is the enemy winning?! Why are God's kids dying so some gangbanger can make a few bucks?"

Jill saw his anger at the terrible things that happened, walked over to Eli, and put her arms around his neck. "Remember the song you told me used to go through your mind when you were on the mound?"

Eli smiled. "You mean 'Secret Ambition'?"

"That's the one," was the sweet answer from Jill.

Eli smiled. "I guess reaching all of our Father's kids is what he wants: The ones who have messed up, the victims, and the bad guys. And it all has to be done for God's kids."

"Eli, the one thing you can count on is that the enemy is going to do everything he can to stop you. Jamaal is going to do some of the most stupid stuff you can imagine. But he is the key. When the garbage comes against him, because of the choice he is making for Christ, that's when your 'Secret Ambition' will come out," Jill said.

"That's when you really have to see Father's face to be able to minister to him and all those kids who look up to him," Jill said in a firm yet sweet voice.

Eli, shaking his head, pointed out, "It's like this. He has been used as a tool of the enemy for so long, and he became drunk with the power it provided him. Now that Christ has a firm hold on him, he is starting to experience what real power feels like. The real power of God himself wins by rebuilding lives, not destroying them. He has destroyed lives, yet the power he now possesses, through the Holy Spirit, is going to amaze him. Frankly, the power of the Holy Spirit still amazes me," Eli said.

Eli continued, "Sweetheart, it's been a really long, tough day. What do you say we turn in a bit early tonight?"

Jill got a sly smile on her face. "What do you say we go to bed a little early and get up a little early in the morning? We do have a lot to accomplish tomorrow."

Eli just smiled as he took his bride's hand and headed to bed.

The next morning, the phone was buzzing beside Eli and Jill's bed.

Jill grabbed the phone, "Good morning."

Eli could hear Jill talking to the desk officer from the jail.

"Yes, officer, Eli is right here." She handed the phone to Eli, giving him a light kiss good morning.

"I hate getting woken up early," grumbled Eli.

She smiled and said, "You'll never change."

Eli took the phone and said, "This is Eli."

The answer from the other end was, "This is officer Quartermain. Jamaal got jumped last night. He is asking for you."

Eli shook his head in disgust. "Wonder what he did to get that treatment?"

Eli looked over at his sweetie and kissed her gently. "I have to go and check on Jamaal. I'll be back soon."

Jill smiled ever so sweetly. "God has given you Jamaal for a reason. You better get down there and find out what is going on."

With that, Eli got up and hit the shower.

Coming out of the shower, he smelled the bacon and eggs that Jill had prepared for him. He sat down, Jill poured the coffee, and they started to discuss what could have happened. Eli finally said, "Jill, you know what? All of this is mere conjecture. I think I just have to go down there and get the straight scoop."

Jill responded, "Eli, would you like me to go with you?"

"That would be great!" Eli answered. Eli was hoping Jill was going to ask. "Sometimes a woman's view can help with the situation," he added.

Eli then waited as Jill got in the shower. Jill came out dressed in modest shorts and a shirt that would not draw undue attention to her by the inmates of the jail.

As they arrived, Eli and Jill went to the desk sergeant. "Eli, are you here to see Jamaal?" the desk sergeant asked.

"That's right," Eli answered.

She hit the buzzer and sent the message to send Jamaal up.

"What happened?" Jill asks gently.

Jamaal blinked back tears. "These dudes called me out. I told them I would not fight as I am now serving Him who sent me to work to see lives changed by Him. I was speaking of Christ. Then one of them hit me and said, 'I don't see Christ defending you now.' Then another one hit me and asked the same question, then another, then another."

Eli got a concerned look on his face.

"Eli, I am not done," Jamaal interjected. "They were done beating me when the guards broke it up. Later, Lud, one of the guys, asked why I did not fight back. I told him that I was done breaking heads. I just wanted to see Christ break hearts."

Eli responded, "What happened next?"

"He accepted Christ," Jamaal said with a broad smile his white teeth showing so brightly the room lit up.

Eli smiled as he said, "Man, you had me worried. How are the guys treating you now?"

"They call me Preach!" was the quick proud answer from Jamaal.

Thumbnail spoke into his ear, "Jamaal, you are doing it right."

Jamaal started looking around. "Who said that?"

"Who said what?" was Eli's questioning response.

Just then, Thumbnail suggested to Jamaal, "Why not ask Eli if he would come in here and teach a Bible study?"

Jamaal shook his head. "I think you're supposed to teach a Bible study in here. What do you think?"

Eli got a questioning look on his face and said, "I will have to pray on that one. I think Pastor Johnson would be a better fit, but I will pray about it."

Eli then added, "By the way, our first game is Wednesday night. You gonna be ready?"

Jamaal looked at Eli with a broad smile, "You know it, buddy. You know it."

10
The Father's Love

IT WAS FIVE fifty in the morning. Eli had already reset the alarm twice. It went off for the third time. Jill sat up in bed, her hair mussed from sleeping. "Eli, I think you have a lot of things to get ready for your game today, do you not?"

Eli opened one eye, looked at his beloved, and said, "I am going back to sleep for a few more minutes."

Jill shook her head. "I don't mind being woken up, knowing you have a great many things to accomplish for God's kingdom. One thing I won't abide by is being woke up three times when you should be up already!" With that, she threw the covers off of Eli, stuck her cold foot in his back, and pushed him out of the bed onto the carpeted floor. She stated, "Mister, it's time to get your butt up and get working on that which Father created you to do. Now get to work!"

Eli pulled himself up off the floor, looked at his sweet bride smiling at him from under the warm covers, shook his head, and walked toward the bathroom.

He started the water, waited for it to warm. He got the heat just right and climbed in.

Eli had his back to the curtain. He had his face covered with soap. Suddenly the water was ice cold. Jill had turned the cold water on as Eli did not have his usual thirty minutes to spend in the shower but needed to get in and out quickly.

Eli screamed, "I sure like being married to you!" as he quickly jumped away from the freezing cold water.

⚾ ⚾ ⚾

Eli asked, "Sweetheart, what's on your agenda today?"

Jill responded, "Corrine and I are going to spend the day at the spa and then join Sam and yourself for dinner at Hampton's Grill at about seven o'clock."

"That should work. Are you two coming to the game at four?" Eli asked.

"Of course! Then after the game, you get Jamaal back to jail and join us for a night on the town," Jill said with a wink and a grin.

"Now, you have to get to work, and I am going back to bed for a couple of hours. It's too early for me!" Jill said, smiling, as she headed back to bed.

Eli walked to the kitchen, poured himself a cup of coffee, and saw his Bible sitting on the table. He said, "Okay, Father, what do you have for me today?" He opened the good book to Romans 5:1: "Since we are justified by faith we have peace with God through our Lord Jesus Christ." As he read this verse over and over, lights started to go on inside his head.

"It's not anything we do, it's Christ!" He smiled, closed the Bible slowly, and repeated to himself, "It's not anything we do, it's Christ. We just trust Christ."

It was now seven o'clock in the morning. He picked up the phone and called Sam. "Sam, I have just read Romans 5:1."

⚾ ⚾ ⚾

Father looked over at Peter and said, "Finally, the truth is starting to sink in. I have been leading Eli for years. He has always loved me, but now he really understands this truth. It is great when my kids finally get the truth."

⚾ ⚾ ⚾

"We have a full team of guys. We cannot neglect the training of any of these guys because one of them is in jail. Here's the deal. On Monday mornings, let's pass the word that we will buy breakfast for anyone who wishes to take part in our Bible study," Eli said, shaking his head. "There is a lot of truth for all of us to learn. We need a disciplined way of doing it. I say we talk to Pastor Johnson and see if he will teach it. At the same time, we will talk to him about a study in the jail that Jamaal can take part in."

Sam, still trying to get awake, shook his head. "Eli, let me get some coffee in me, and I will call you back." With that, Sam looked over at his sweet Corrine sleeping next to him. He crawled out of bed, put his shorts on, and walked into the bathroom.

He then went to the kitchen, put some coffee on, and opened his Bible to Romans 5:1. He thought to himself, *Wonder what got Eli so excited this morning?*

As he read it, the simple truth hit him like a ton of bricks. "Simple faith in Christ. That's all it takes, is that simple faith in Christ. I know what we are going to put on our jerseys now. Romans 5:1. We are justified by faith, and that faith has to be in Christ, who paid the price for our justification. Jesus paid the price, I knew that. But these guys have to get it. Wonder if we could name our team 'Romans 5:1 Raiders'?"

With that, he called Eli back. "Eli, what do you think of the idea of calling our team the Romans 5:1 Raiders?"

Eli got real quiet. "I think you have got something there. We are going into the area that the enemy has controlled for years, and Christ is gonna use us to take it back. Our justification comes, not by anything that we do, but through Christ and what he has done."

Sam smiled.

● ● ●

That afternoon at the game, Sam and Eli called the team together for a meeting.

Sam said, "Guys, Eli and I have been discussing the name of this team. We think it ought to be called the Romans 5:1 Raiders."

Jamaal spoke up, "What does Romans 5:1 say?"

Eli interjected, "Romans 5:1 said, 'We are justified by faith.' That's the only justification we need. We are going to attack the enemy of man and draw God's people back to Christ. This team, win or lose, is going to be one of prayer and power."

Locud, one of Jamaal's teammates, asked, "What if I don't believe in all the prayer mumbo jumbo?"

Eli again simply smiled. "Watch, keep an open mind, and see what God is going to do in the lives of those around you."

Eli looked at Sam and said, "Sam, would you pray so we can get these guys warmed up?"

Sam prayed, "Father, keep us safe, and may what we do as a team honor you in the name of Christ our Lord, Amen."

Eli commanded, "Okay, guys, warm it up."

The team went out to warm up.

Eli's two pitchers, Sam Adams and Thadius, were both warming up.

Sammy had been listening to Eli and had been practicing exactly what Eli had shown him. Eli had set him up to be his power closer, and Thadius was going to be his pitcher with his finesse and control.

Thumbnail said to Jamaal, "Today, you hit a home run; hit it to the right field over the fence. There will be a little boy named Joshua on the other side, watching."

Jamaal shook his head and asked himself, *Again that voice, who is that voice?*

It was the second inning. Jamaal was batting. He looked over to the right field fence.

He saw a little boy standing there all alone. The pitcher, Ron Simpson, wound up to throw a fast ball. The ball came in about 80 mph, and Jamaal sent it over the right field fence. It was a home run.

The little boy ran over and got the ball. The game went on, and the Raiders won.

After the game, the little boy brought the ball up to Jamaal. His mother was with him.

"Mr. Jamaal, can I get your autograph?" the little boy asked.

"Little boy, how old are you?" asked Jamaal.

"I am ten," Came the answer from the child's sweet voice.

That hit Jamaal like a ton of bricks. That was the age of the little boy who died because of Jamaal giving him the meth. Jamaal smiled, signed the ball, and smiled at his mom.

Jamaal walked over and got into Sam's BMW and sobbed the entire way back to jail.

Thumbnail said to him, "Jamaal, you are forgiven by our Father for what you have done, but He will let it haunt you for the rest of your years so you will keep working to get other little guys not to do it and stop those who want to destroy young lives."

Eli walked over to the sidelines as Michael Howard walked up to him and said, "Eli, can we have lunch tomorrow? I have a plan drawn up for the construction company that I think will meet your approval. As I see it, by using primarily the ghetto kids, you can have an extremely good return on investment. With the money this could bring in, we could really have a war on poverty. With your help, the people that the enemy controls through poverty would see that poverty quickly come to an end."

That night Sam and Corrine were at Eli and Jill's for supper. Jill had made mashed potatoes, catfish, turnip greens, and a dessert of the best peach cobbler a girl from Duluth, Minnesota, could think of making. They were all sitting around the table when Sam brought up, "What is this I hear about you helping start a construction company? Did you think we were going to let you have all the fun?"

Eli shook his head. "Sam, you were there when I first started talking about this with Mike Howard."

Sam laughed. "Yeah, I know. I was just giving you a hard time. How much money are you gonna need? I have about an extra twenty million dollars I can throw into the mix."

Eli looked puzzled. "I had no idea you were interested in getting involved with this project. I trust you have talked it over with Corrine?"

The response was so quick from Corrine that Eli about fell off his chair. "Eli, it's my idea. I have a master's degree in business from UCIA. I am just the person you need running this company. And you, my friend, I hear you have a promise that you made your mom about getting back in school. She reminded me of that today," was Corrine's answer.

Jill added, "Mister, you made your mom a promise when you went pro instead of college. Keep it."

Eli ran his hand through his hair, over his face, across his chin. "Where did all this stuff about college come from? My investments make more money than we can ever spend, why college?"

Jill responded, "Eli, a promise is a promise unless your mother releases you from it. You're stuck. You have to go to college. Think back to the promise you made to my dad. You would not break that. How is this different?"

Eli shook his head. Suddenly a light went on. "I could take computer classes from a Bible school, learn the Word that could help even more in the ministry Father has put us in," he said.

After dinner, the guys did the noble thing and cleared the table. They did a quick cleanup of the pans and stacked the dishwasher. As they returned to the living room, they saw their brides sitting with big smiles on their faces. They both had terry cloth robes on.

"We decided to go for a swim while you guys were so graciously doing the dishes. Care to join us?" Jill asked ever so sweetly.

Both men smiled and said, in unison, "Let's do it."

As the four of them were floating around the pool, Eli asked, "What schools offer online Bible courses?"

Corrine responded, "I know Moody does, and so does Northwestern College out of Minneapolis."

Jill added, "You're serious about this?"

"Yeah, babes, I am! I made a promise. I have to follow through on it."

The next morning, Eli and Jill made the seven o'clock mass then hopped over to the church in the ghetto to hear Pastor Johnson preach.

As they walked into the church, the members of the church all looked over at Eli and Jill.

After the service, Eli asked Pastor Johnson, "I am looking for a Bible school that I can take classes online from, any suggestions?"

"How about Fullerton? It's close, so you can contact your professors if you need to. And it's a good school. It may shake up some of your Catholic doctrine, but it will make you defend what you believe, and that's always a good thing."

As Eli and Jill got in the Caddy, Eli said, "I think that is an avenue that I can explore. As a matter of fact, it is one I will explore."

Eli pulled the car over, took out his cell phone, entered Fullerton as a contact, and then continued driving.

As Eli was driving, he drove right by their condo's driveway and kept heading down the street. Jill got a puzzled look on her face. "Where are we going?"

Eli's quick response was, "To jail, hun."

Jill said, "Mister McBrien, are you going to talk to Jamaal about getting involved in an online Bible school?"

With a smile, Eli acknowledged his bride. "Babes, you read me like a book."

A few minutes later, they were at the county jail. Eli walked in. Before he could ask, the desk sergeant had called for Jamaal to be brought to the visiting area.

Jamaal came out and asked Eli, "What brings you here today? You never come on Sundays."

Eli answered, "It is quite simple. I need a study partner."

Jill looked at Eli, smiled, and nodded her head, leaned over to him, and whispered, "I had a feeling that is exactly what you would do."

Eli smiled as he told Jamaal about the course he was going to take. "If you're interested, I could see if I could arrange a scholarship for you."

The answer he got from Jamaal surprised him. "Eli, I can't read."

"You can't read? I saw you reading the Bible," was the immediate response.

"That's right. The teachers did not want to deal with me. They just kept passing me on." He continued, "The only thing I am able to read is the Bible. God did a miracle, and I can read his Word, but everything else is still messed up."

Eli got a puzzled look on his face. He walked over to the library in the jail and pulled a commentary off the shelf, handed it to Jamaal, and asked him to read it. Jamaal could not. Then he handed him the pocket testament he had with him. His reading was perfect.

Eli ran his hands through his hair. "This presents another problem. I am going to have a teacher here for you next week. You will learn to read. When I was in grade school, I had problems of my own. Jamaal, I am dyslexic."

"What?" was Jamal's surprised question.

"Jamaal, I have struggled with this my whole life. I am sending a specialist here tomorrow to help you learn to read."

Eli walked across the room. Jill could see the anger in his face. "These schools just don't care, the parents don't care!" He looked at Jamaal, "Your mom excluded."

Jill saw that Eli was getting very upset. "Jill, my mom was great! You saw how involved she was. Remember when that teacher tried to get you and I to do things on stage we should not have in Romeo and Juliet? Why don't these schools understand what has to be done for these kids and do it?"

Eli continued, "Why is it that kids get to be this age and cannot even read a street sign? How can they ever accomplish anything meaningful in life? I just want to make a difference in these young people's lives. The only way that is going to happen is by taking the time to have them learn how to read."

Eli and Jill spent some time with Jamaal teaching him some basics in reading and handling his dyslexia. Eli understood that his being able to read only the Bible was something that would help big time, but to really understand the Word, he had to be able to read the scholars that knew the history of the situations that presented themselves.

They also came to realize that he was really bright and caught on extremely quickly.

On the way home, they spent the time discussing how they were going to deal with the situation. When they got home they walked into their condo and flopped down on the couch. Then they just looked at each other.

Eli said, "Hun, I have one hundred million dollars in the bank, yet, I don't think all that money is enough to help all these kids. We need to really seek Father on this one to get his guidance how to reach these kids."

With that, they took hands and started to pray. They sought their heavenly Father's face on how to help the kids.

As they were praying, a light went on inside of Eli's head. "Why don't we start a tutoring center?" He asked.

Jill smiled. "I had a feeling Father was showing you just how to do it as well," she said in tone of total support.

Eli got a smile on his face. "I think I know just what I am going to name this. I will name it after my grandma, The Helen McBrien Tutoring Center!"

"Eli, that was the first time you have ever mentioned her to me," Jill stated in a questioning tone.

"Babes, this woman was an old time Pentecostal. She thought my mom marrying a Catholic was not the right thing to do. She showed us kids a great deal of love, but when we would stay with her, she would take us to her church, Calvary Temple. That, my dear, was my first real encounter with Christ. I stayed with her for a couple of weeks in Duluth, Minnesota. What an interesting experience. She taught me a lot as a young child."

Eli continued, "I think it would be a great way of honoring the woman, who had so much to do with me being who I am."

Jill got a look of total respect and admiration for Eli on her face. "Hun, how do we start this?"

Eli smiled. "Like this." Then he picked up his cell and gave Pastor Stuart Johnson a call. "Stu, I have an idea. We need to set up a tutoring center. There are way too many kids falling through the cracks in the system. Do you think you can set it up for say, $250,000, and we will go from there?"

Stu was just getting the cobwebs out of his head. He had been taking a nap.

"Eli, can you send me an e-mail detailing just exactly what you are looking to start here? I think we can accomplish it for a whole lot less than that, and you have to be able to let the community get involved and help finance this. By doing that, they will take ownership in it."

Eli looked over at Jill and said, "Babes, these kids are flunking out of school because no one cared enough to roll up their sleeves and help them learn. We need to start rolling up ours. I can see now why Father had me working so hard as a child, but I also understand why the arm went out so early."

⚾ ⚾ ⚾

The Father looked over at Peter and said, "He gets it. He understands that everything I do, I do for a reason. They don't have to understand it when it happens, but in time they will."

⚾ ⚾ ⚾

Jill walked over to Eli, put her arms around his neck, pulled him in close, and gave him a passionate kiss that only a loving wife could give her husband.

The excitement in Eli was evident. "Wow! What did I do to deserve that?"

Jill smiled and said, "Mister, your Father's love is working inside you like no one else I have ever known. I just wanted to show my approval for all that you open yourself to let Father do."

11
Real Power

THE NEXT MORNING, the alarm went off at six o'clock sharp. Eli started to reach over to shut it off. Jill grabbed his hand and kissed it, leaned over to him, and said in a most seductive voice, "Mister, it's time to get up, you have a very busy day."

Eli's response was quick and sure, "Hun, I hate mornings. Always have, always will." With that, he gave his bride a kiss and got up.

Eli walked to the kitchen, put the bacon on, slid the bread into the toaster, and made the coffee. The toast popped up. He buttered it with sweet butter and cinnamon sugar. Jill walked out of the shower just as Eli is putting the rose in the small vase in front of her plate.

⚾ ⚾ ⚾

Peter looked over at Father and said, "Father, you really have created a loving couple here."

The Father's gentle answer explained something profound to Peter. "Pete, what you see working in their marriage is a principle that I put forth in my Word. When the wife respects her husband to the level that Jill respects Eli, then the natural response for Eli is to love his wife. It's the whole love and respect thing. It's a circle thing. Guard that circle and marriages succeed. Break it, and that's what happens to the marriage, it breaks," the great I Am said.

Peter responded in one word: "Wow!"

Eli and Jill finished their breakfast. Jill cooed as she said, "Thanks, sweetheart, that was great!"

"Eli, I realize you would love to spend your day with me, but you do have to get the team ready for the game Wednesday night. You also have a construction company to get off the ground, and you have a hospital to build. So, my loving gift, my stud, get that cute behind of yours out of here and get to work! I have to change the nursery colors to blue."

Eli stopped cold in his tracks. "What?"

Jill smiled at Eli, "Get out of here, and get to it mister!"

Eli kissed her again and walked out just as Sam drove up.

As Eli got into the car with Sam, he had a quizzical look on his face.

Sam asked, "What's going on there, bud?"

Eli shaking his head responded, "Jill, as I was walking out of the house, said she had to change the colors of the nursery to blue."

"Ahhh," was Sam's response.

"And you're coming to work why?" Sam continued.

Eli shook his head. "She kicked me outta the house before I had a chance to ask any questions."

Sam stated, "We have a meeting with Mike on the new construction company. Then we have a meeting with the Mayor of LA to start talking about a new hospital in the Watts area. Then we have to meet with the City League about getting this thing off the ground and work on scheduling. Then—"

Eli interrupted, "Hey man, let me take a breath! And that's all before lunch?"

Sam answered, "Has to be, we have practice this afternoon, and then we meet with Mike again to discuss the coffee shop in the church I said we would help fund."

"We?" Was Eli's response.

Sam got a grin on his face that said, "Man, have I got another surprise for you."

"Oh yeah! I also got ahold of your attorney in Duluth. What do you think of a company called M&S Enterprises?"

Eli got another quizzical look on his face. "What's this about?"

"It's about protecting our families in case something bad happens with all these things we are getting involved with," came Sam's quick answer.

"Ah, I see the big picture," Eli answered quickly. "Have him draw up the papers for the incorporation," was Eli's answer.

Arriving at Mike Howard's office, they walked inside. Mike arose from his desk to great them. In the next hour, Sam told Mike about Corrine's education, which impressed him greatly.

Eli stated excitedly, "Mike, we have also drawn up the papers for the incorporation of this enterprise."

Eli continued, "Corrine will be the head of the business arm of this thing. You will handle the day-to-day operations, and Sam and I have a baseball team to run."

Mike got a look of total approval on his face as he said, "So I see you folks really do have all of your ducks in a row. I think I am going to enjoy working with you. I can only imagine what this operation will look like in ten years."

The next day, they had all the papers drawn up, signed, and sent off.

🌕 🌕 🌕

Pete looked over at the Father. "Father, you have Sam and Eli involved with many different things at the same time. How are they going to keep everything straight?"

The Father smiled as He gave his most gracious answer, "Remember when Eli was a young lad, just starting out in baseball, how I told you he would be the best pitcher ever, and I would get the credit?"

Peter nodded.

The Father continued, "Well, he is the best pitcher ever, and he gave the credit will be given to me always. I can trust him. They will accomplish great things, but you know what? The son I am creating that is going to be born shortly to them will be a greater all-around baseball player but will never be the pitcher his dad was. The hospital that I am going to have built will be one of the best in the world, and out of the tutoring center is going to come some of the greatest minds known to man. At the same time, their families will flourish in the love and caring only I can give," the Father said, smiling.

◗ ◗ ◗

Eli, Sam, Corrine, and Jill were sitting across from Mike Howard thinking, "*What did we get ourselves into?*"

Corrine spoke first. "Mike, what kind of money are we talking here to get this thing up and running?"

Mike got an impish grin on his face. "How much you got?"

Eli and Sam said in unison, "We will give you five million dollars a piece."

Corrine stated, "Mike, I want you to bid out the business. We must show a profit. We cannot pour the money down a hole. No one gains when we do that. We have been given a stewardship here. God, our Father, has allowed us to have access to a lot of cash. We dare not waste it. When you bring me a bid, I am going to check it to make sure it will make sense. If it does, then we get the business. The retained earnings will go into a fund. When a hundred million dollars is in the reserves, then we build the hospital. But here is the biggest challenge to us: we must use ghetto residence for the work crews and to get the biggest impact we can. How long is it going to take you to get a trained crew to take care of this?" She asked.

"Corrine, you do realize the vast majority of people in the ghetto are black, don't you?" Mike said with a questioning tone.

Corrine shook her head. "And your point is?"

She continued, "If they are okay with a cute blond as one of their bosses, then I don't care. What are they, a bunch of racists?"

Mike just shook his head. "Where do I find the workers?" Was his question.

⚾ ⚾ ⚾

Pete looked at the Father and asked, "Father, how are you going to get over the mistrust that is in the ghetto? How do you get them to trust?"

Father just stated, "Stay tuned, Pete.

"Let me just say this: truth will be triumphant."

⚾ ⚾ ⚾

The next day, Wednesday, it was game day for the team.

Eli arrived at the jail to pick up Jamaal. Jamaal came out in orange, cuffed as usual. Jamaal had a huge smile on his face. Eli asked, "Hey man, what's going on?"

Jamaal's grin got even bigger. "I led a brother to Christ last night!" Came the response.

The excitement that went through Eli's whole being was evident. "Jamaal, that's great, fantastic! Tell me about it!" Came Eli's quick response.

As they walked to Eli's car, the excitement could be seen building within Jamaal. "It was like this. Two brothers were fighting. I stepped in between them, told them to stop, and I would show them some real power."

Eli smiled, "And?"

"I pretty much told them the same thing you said to me on the hood of your Challenger the first time I met you." There was excitement radiating from Jamaal as he spoke.

As they approached the baseball field, Jamaal asked Eli, "Man, how did you ever learn to pitch so well?"

Eli smiled and said, "Secret Ambition."

"What?" Was Jamaal's only response.

"Listen to this," Eli said as he put Michael W. Smith's CD into his player.

"Wow!" Was all Jamaal could say. "What was your secret ambition?" he responded.

Eli smiled as he said, "My ambition has always, and will always be, to reach kids with the power of Christ. To have them understand that the Father has their back in everything that they do. For them to not be scared, to reach out to those around them with the love and power that Christ, with the Father, brings into any situation."

Jamaal smiled as he understood. That was exactly what Eli was doing. By following the passion that the Heavenly Father, through the Son, has placed within Eli's heart.

12

Even Being Forgiven…

JILL, NINE MONTHS pregnant, was cuddled up to Eli's back in bed, and Eli felt the baby kick him. He smiled, "I love you, babes, I really do!"

Jill kissed his back. "Love you too, my sweet!" she said in a sweet, cooing voice.

It was three in the morning. Jill suddenly felt the pains of labor starting. She then whispered in Eli's ear, "Sweetheart, it's time."

Eli grumbled and answered, "Time for what? Go back to sleep."

The not so quiet voice of his beloved came back. "Wake up, or you'll miss the birth of your son!"

Eli sat straight up in bed. "What!?"

Jill's answer was quick. "It's time to go."

With that, Eli jumped into high gear, grabbed her stuff, and headed out of the house, then remembered one very important thing: Jill. He turned and ran back into the house to get her. He rushed into the house, smiled a sheepish smile, and helped his very pregnant bride out to the Escalade.

Eli started the engine and headed to the hospital. Once again, he was driving way over the speed limit and saw the lights as they came on behind him. "Nooo! Not again!" Eli said as he pulled over. "Every time I speed and the lights come on."

The officer came to Jill's side of the car. Jill opened her window. "Please, officer, I'm in labor."

The officer's reply was quick and to the point. "Which hospital? Follow me!" Following the officer with his lights flashing and siren blaring, Eli was able to stay close so they could go through the lights as they rushed to the hospital.

Arriving at LA Memorial Hospital, Jill was rushed to the delivery room. Eli parked the SUV and got to the room just in time to see his son born. "Sweetheart, he's beautiful! He gets his great looks from his mom."

Jill smiled and said, "His mom is not feeling so beautiful right now."

Eli responded, "You're the most beautiful woman in the world right now! I love you sooo much!" Next came the question that would cause a bit of conflict for them. "What should we name him?" Eli asked.

Jill said, "Let me rest a bit, then we will figure it out." Mom and baby are taken to their room. Eli walked to the waiting room where he got some much needed sleep as well.

A few hours later, Jill woke and asked for her son, then for Eli.

The nurse walked into the waiting room, where Eli was sleeping like a baby, nudged him and said, "Jill is asking for you."

Eli got up and walked into the room. "Morning, Babes!" he said as he walked in.

Nursing the baby, she smiled back at Eli. "Morning, Sweetie. I think it's time we name this little guy, don't you?"

Eli smiled and gave his idea. "I like the name Herman."

The look on Jill's face could have stopped a train. "Herman?" she asked, with a tone that said, "*Are you nuts?*"

Eli answered, "That was my great-grandfather's name. My grandfather told me that when my great-grandma went into labor with my grandfather, she was on the way to Grandpa Herman Johnson's funeral. He never got to meet him."

Jill answered with, "I was thinking of something a bit more traditional, like Michael, or John." Just then, Thumbnail hopped on Jill's shoulder and said, "Imagine a pitcher who can hit and who is a great base stealer being named the great Herman McBrien! It would have a cool ring to it!"

Jill looked at Eli and smiled. "You know, hun, I can see the great Herman McBrien as a baseball player that will also be a great servant of our Father in heaven."

Eli kissed Jill on the top of her head, much like he did when they were dating in purity, smiled his warm smile, and said, "Babes, this kid has a great mom. Hopefully, his dad can be as great."

Jill let's out a laugh. "Eli, you're already a great father. All you have to do is follow the example that is given to you, and you will be a great dad."

Eli got a puzzled look on his face. "Example?" he asked.

Jill smiled even broader. "The example of our Father in heaven; His Word laid out a pretty good example of what a good father looks like, does it not?"

Eli got a sheepish grin on his face. "Oh yeah, that Father!" he said laughing.

Eli took Jill's hand. "Lets pray. I want to start the life of this little guy out right. I know we have prayed all through the pregnancy, but I really feel like we need to pray now."

* * *

Thumbnail got a huge smile on his face, "I did good again, did I not?"

The Father looked over at Peter and then at Thumbnail. "Thumbnail, let me ask you a simple question. Who puts thoughts into your mind?"

Thumbnail's face turned bright red. "You do Father! I do apologize, but can I still get excited about being used?"

Father chuckled. "That, Thumbnail, you can get excited about. And it even blesses me when you are excited about it."

* * *

Eli prayed. "Father, we come to you through your Son, Jesus, the Christ. We ask that you touch the son you have given to us. Dwell within him so that he will know you through your Spirit and never let him go. Draw him to you in everything you do with him through his life. Use him to touch not only thousands of people but millions. In the name of your Son, Jesus the Christ. Amen."

Jill pulled Eli down to herself and kissed him ever so gently. Eli returned the kiss with a whole lot of passion. As they pulled apart, the nurse walked in, and one could almost see the angels around them singing. Eli said, "I love being married to you, Jill McBrien."

Father looked over to Peter and said, "Pete, you know I have said there will never be as great a pitcher as Eli, and there won't. There will never be as great an all-around player as Herman McBrien, and his fame will reach millions."

Two days later, they took Herman home. Sam and Corrine had been decorating the nursery. They walked in and the room has LA's stuff all over the walls. There was a child's baseball glove on the dresser. The look of excitement on Jill's face amazed even Eli.

"Eli, did you do this?" was the question from Jill.

"Not me." Just then, there was a knock at the door. Eli walked over to answer it, looked through the peep hole, and saw Corrine and Sam standing there. He opened the door and said, "Hey guys, welcome."

Corrine, with excitement in her voice, said, "Do you like what we did for little Herman?"

Jill smiled, "It's great! How did you get in?"

Sam smiled at Eli.

Thumbnail jumped up and down on Eli's shoulder. Eli looked at his shoulder trying to figure out what kept bouncing.

Thumbnail just smiled and kept jumping up and down with the excitement that came from being on a winning team.

Eli looked at his sweet bride, "Hun, I have to be honest. They said they wanted something special for our son, so I gave them the key. I had no idea what they were gonna do."

Sam smiled at the two of them and with a somewhat snide retort. "Ya! Eli is clueless again," he said, laughing.

Corrine interjected, "Boys, play nice," as she laughed.

Eli took Herman from his mom as the phone rang. Corrine walked over and answered the phone. "Eli, its Jamaal."

Eli handed the baby to Sam. "Jamaal, how goes it, man?" Eli answered, with joy in his voice.

Jamaal responded, "Eli, there was a group from First Church in tonight teaching a Bible study. It's a pretty black church from the burbs someplace. They want me to come and talk about what drugs do to people. Next Sunday night is when they want me. Can we make it?"

Eli looked over at Sam. Sam nodded and told Eli, "I'll cover you on it, bro. You stay here with your bride and son."

Eli said, "Jamaal, Sam will cover me on this one. We will get it done. I will be staying here with Jill and Herman."

Jamaal lets out a yell, "You had your son?! Great, man! I am sooo proud of you! You finally did it!"

The phone had been on speaker, and everyone laughed.

Eli was just standing there, smiling and shaking his head. He chuckled a bit and said, "Know what? This kid may turn out great in spite of me."

The Father looked over at Peter and said, "Pete, little Herman is great because of what my Son did. I wish people would just think about who they are, in my Son, and walk in it. The greatness that they all could accomplish is an amazing thing to contemplate. I give my people ideas, and they do nothing with them. Eli was given gifts, and he used them. Herman was given gifts, and he will do things with them because I implanted in his father the drive to make his gifts useful in my kingdom. The way he is using the gifts I have given him now is more important than the fact that he was, and always be, the best pitcher baseball had ever seen."

Peter looked at the Father with a look of total admiration on his face, and said, "Father, what gifts are you talking about?"

Father nodded, showing his total love for Peter. "Pete, his character and influence and willingness to use the fortunes I gave him to build my kingdom. That, my son, is what makes him greater after his playing days than when he was playing. His willingness to work with those who have nothing and to give them hope is what makes him greater now than when he was playing."

Thumbnail whispered to Eli, "Tell Jamaal that he does not get to see baby Herm until his sentence is finished."

Eli shook his head, "What?" he asked.

All those in the room looked at Eli as if to say, "Who are you talking to?"

Thumbnail ordered, "Tell him."

So Eli told Jamaal that he would not be able to meet Herm until every day of his sentence was served.

Jamaal's answer showed just how dumbfounded he was. "What? You're kidding, right?"

Eli responded, "You know, it's like this. You broke the law. We will tell Herm about you as he grows, but you will not get to meet him until the day you walk out of jail a free man."

Peter looked over at the Father with a quizzical look on his face. "Why, Father, would you have it set up this way?"

"Pete, I have to give people hope. I use whatever I need to as a motivator to reach those who would have no hope. Jamaal would be in prison for the rest of his life if it had not been for Eli and Sam. Aaron will give him the coaching he needs as a hitter, and he will become a great slugger. A lot of great things are going to happen in his life the day he walks out of jail. But while he is there, for the next nine years, I am going to use him to reach hundreds of men who come through there with the power that comes through my Son, Jesus Christ. I am going to use him as an example of how to touch those around themselves with My Holy Spirit that dwells within them."

Eli heard the huge disappointment in Jamaal's voice. Eli thought, *Maybe, I could let him…*

Then Thumbnail piped in, "Eli, don't even think of it. He hurt kids. There is no way Father is going to bless you breaking His will on this one."

Eli looked around, but he knew, somehow, the Father was speaking to him. Jamaal was pleading with him. Eli's answer was quick and to the point, "Man, it's like this! You hurt kids! You have to pay the price for hurting kids! And part of that price is not seeing our son until you have served every day of the ten years. I am sorry, but that's the way it's going to be."

13
Church League Lessons

IT WAS ONE year later. The Church League that Eli and Sam had put together had been a huge success. Kids had been taken off the streets, friendships had been built, and the League had drawn the attention of both colleges and pros. Players were getting college scholarships, and a few had been picked up by minor league teams.

Eli and Herm were playing ball in the living room. Jill walked over to see them playing catch and smiled to herself. She said, "Throw the ball to Mommy."

Herm wound up and let it fly. The ball hit Jill in the chest. The look of surprise on her face was telling. "Guess he really does have a pretty good arm, eh!" she said with a smile.

Eli responded, "Well, he is his father's son!" as he chuckled with a smile.

Herm ran over, threw his arms around his mom, smiled, and kissed her on the cheek.

Jill smiled, looked over at Eli, and thought back to their dating days. "Another great holy kiss from a young man that I love," she said.

Eli smiled, walked over, and gave them both a light kiss. "Holy kisses are the best."

The phone rang. Eli walked over to answer it. "Hello."

"Eli, Sam here. We have an issue. Not really a problem, but an issue."

"What's that?" was Eli's questionable answer.

"Jamaal called. He's got twenty inmates who want to accept Christ as their Savior. Ten of them get out of jail next week. He wants us to help them find churches," Sam said.

Sam added, "Half of them are Muslims."

Eli, standing in his kitchen with a coffee cup on the counter, responded, "Tell me they're not on some watch list, please!"

Sam answered, "Not at all, just Muslims."

Eli responded again, "Just get their names. I'll have my friends at the police and Homeland Security run a check, and then we will figure out what course of action to take. If they check out, I see no reason not to get them hooked into a church. Also, find out what they were convicted of."

Sam got the names of the men, who were Muslims, who are claiming to be Christians and e-mailed them to Eli's phone. Eli immediately sent them on to Homeland Security. They were all positive on the terror watch list.

Jacob Lloyd of the FBI called Eli at home. "Eli, these guys are on the watch list. We thought we had them but could not get the evidence we needed for a conviction, so we had to drop charges."

Eli got a concerned look on his face. "What do you want us to do?"

Jacob responded, "We just want you to play along with them. You're a pretty astute believer. You will be able to see if their conversion to Christ was real. Just go with what your gut, intuition, and the Holy Spirit tells you." He added one more thing, "Do not, I repeat, DO NOT tell Jamaal what's going on!"

☙ ☙ ☙

The Father looked to Peter then to the Son and commanded, "I want a legion of angels around these guys at all times. My Word says that even the elect would be taken in. That will not happen here."

Peter responded, "So these are bad guys, right? Tools of the enemy?"

The Father gave a quick response, "No, these men's conversions were real. However, the enemy will try to get them back. If they turn back, they will be more evil than when they started."

☙ ☙ ☙

Eli agreed to the idea, walked over to Jill, and said, "You're not going to believe this! The Muslims are all on the watch list, and they want me to be their snitch and keep an eye on these guys for them."

Jill got a worried look on her face as she said, "Eli, I don't know if I want you to doing this."

Thumbnail jumped on Jill's shoulder. "Don't worry. Father has everything under control. If these guy's conversions are real, they can be a powerful tool in the hands of our Father."

Jill looked over at Eli, shook her head in disbelief, then relaxed, and said, "You're a smart guy. Just promise me you'll be careful."

Eli responded, "Babes, you know I will be. I have a beautiful bride, a great son, and a Heavenly Father who loves us all. In Philippians 4:13 Paul tells us that we always have the victory through Christ who gives us strength. We will win in this situation, and many, many lives will be saved."

Jill looked over at him, smiled, and said, "Sweetheart, you're talking about conversions here, are you not?"

The look on Eli's face was telling as he responded. "Both conversions to Christ and their lives saved so they can reside on this earth a few more years. Jill, I was created for such a time as this; I was created to see those lives saved. Now and for all eternity! Jill, I have to be about our Father's business." With that, Eli walked out to the car, started the engine, and drove down to the jail. He walked in, and the new jailer, Carlos Rodriguez, greeted Eli as he walked in.

"I suppose you need to see Jamaal," was all Carlos said.

Eli answered, "Yup."

Carlos picked up the phone and called to the back to get them to bring Jamaal to the front.

Eli smiled as Jamaal rounded the corner. "Hey there bud, I heard you have some people here who need to accept Christ as their Savior."

Jamaal's smile was so broad even the light bulbs dimmed in comparison.

"Yup, we have talked and talked, and they say they're ready."

Eli got a concerned look on his face as he said, "You don't sound real convinced, my friend."

Jamaal shook his head, "I'm not."

Eli walked over and put his hand on Jamaal's right shoulder. "Let me remind you, no one can say Jesus is Lord except by the Holy Spirit. Jamaal, let's go talk to them, and let me see what the Spirit tells me about them," Eli said. The two men walked back into the cell block to speak with the Muslims in the cell.

Eli asked the leader of the group, "Jamaal tells me you want to become a Christian. Why?"

The leader of the group looked at Eli and said, "My religion is one of fear. You either follow our law or you are killed. There is no love in it, only death and servitude. We see Jamaal and the hope in his eyes. We see the love coming from him to us. We want that love. Tell us how to get it, please?"

Eli looked at Jamaal, and Jamaal looked at Eli. Eli simply stated, "All you have to do is believe, repent, and be baptized into Christ." Then Eli asked them all to pray with him. He led them in a prayer of repentance and asking for forgiveness and surrendering to Christ.

Thumbnail told Eli to tell the men that if they get sucked back into Islam, they will be more evil than when Christ pulled them out.

Eli shook his head a little and told them. "Okay, you guys, remember this. Christ told us about when demons were cast out. If the empty space is not filled with something, then something far worse is going to come back and fill the space. So you need to be filling your mind by reading the Bible and asking for the filling of the Holy Spirit so that empty space in your hearts can be filled with something productive."

Eli turned just as Sam walked in behind him. "Hey man, they're out in three days, the same time as Jamaal's next game. What do you say we have a little party at the game, invite them, and barbecue with the other team?"

Eli got a stern look on his face. "We can do that. I will have a guard here to bring Jamaal back to jail after the game. He is not allowed to take part in such activities."

Sam nodded. "I thought maybe just once they would make an exception."

Eli shook his head. "Look man, he hurt a lot of kids. I won't make an exception. He has five years left, and he will serve them without exception."

Three days later at the game, all of Jamaal's Muslim friends were there.

Jamaal played like a man possessed, possessed by the Holy Spirit that is. He could do nothing wrong, from catching impossible fly balls to hitting home runs.

Eli's son, Herman, saw Jamaal for the first time and asked Jill a simple question. "Who is that big man in the outfield? Is that the man I hear Daddy talking about a lot?"

Jill put her arm around her five-year-old, smiled, and said, "Sure is."

Herman got a slight smile on his face and said, "Can I meet him, Mama?"

Jill smiled, wishing she could say yes, but realized that she and Eli had agreed. Herman would only meet Jamaal after he had served every day of his sentence.

She simply said, "When the time is right, you'll get to meet him. When the time is right."

⚾ ⚾ ⚾

Father looked over at Pete. "I think this little boy is going to push and see what he can talk his mother into. Watch this. Jill won't be pushed."

⚾ ⚾ ⚾

Herman said, "Mom, when is the right time? Why can't I meet him now?"

Thumbnail jumped on Jill's shoulder. "Don't give in on this. He has to learn what authority you have."

Jill got a stern look on her face. "Herm, I said when the time is right. You have to trust Mommy and Daddy on this one," she stated with the authority of one commissioned by God himself.

The look on Herman's face almost melted Jill, but she knew she could not give in.

The Father spoke to Peter. "Herman is learning about my structure and order. It will serve him well when he gets to the big leagues; also, when he serves in the ministry that I have for him."

Peter got a quizzical look on his face. "What ministry?"

The Father chuckled. "Peter, you know I never let on what I am going to do until the time is right."

After the game, the grill came out. The meat was pulled from the coolers, and the cuffs were put on Jamaal's wrists. The look on his face was one of sadness and grief.

Eli walked over to him, put his hand on his shoulder, and said, "Man, you can't stay. You broke man's law, and you pay man's price."

Jamaal looked at Eli and responded, "Man, how about a burger for the ride back?"

Eli shook his head. "You know I can't do that. We step out of line and they will send you away for 140 years, so we play by the rules. When will you learn that?"

Eli led Jamaal back to the police car that would take him back to jail.

Jamaal looked at Eli as he ducked his head to get in the squad car and said, "Eli, if it weren't for you, man, I would probably be dead. Your son is blessed to have a dad that cares enough for him to make sacrifices of his time and love. He is a blessed child. Five more years and I will meet him."

Eli responded, "Thanks for the compliment, man, but know this. Christ will do great things with you. Your future, after these years, looks great. Play by the rules is all you have to do."

14

The Little Red-Haired Boy

THREE YEARS LATER. Jamaal was impressing the other players on the team game in and game out. There was no pitcher in the church league that could strike him out.

Eli and Sam drove up to the jail to pick him up. This day was a bit different than the others. The sky was gray, the temperature was cooler, and it felt like rain. Eli was now thirty, making little Herman nine. Eli looked over at Sam and said, "Little Herm was getting to be quite a slugger. He got a piece of one last night and drove it at least two hundred feet! Not bad for a nine-year-old, eh?"

Sam nodded in agreement, and he stated, "Eli, your kid's gonna be a slugger, but right now, we have also been given a man who is now twenty-seven, top of his form, and we have had scouts looking at him."

Eli responded, "Your point?"

"Next year he is out, suppose you should start pitching to him, make him be able to hit a real pitcher?" Sam responded with a note of excitement in his voice.

The concern became quite evident on Eli's face as he asked, "What's the problem man? What are your issues here?"

A squad car pulled up beside Eli's new BMW SUV, and turned his lights on. Eli pulled over. The officer came to Eli's window. "Mr. McBrien, I know you have a game tonight, but we are worried about Jamaal's safety. I was sent to pull you over so we could talk about this away from Jamaal. The drug lords that Jamaal sent away have put a hit on Jamaal, and we have to try to protect him. We think they are going to make a move on Jamaal soon. We need to keep him low for a while."

The curl on his brow gave away Eli's concern over this statement. "I take it there will be no practice then? But what about the game? Is it still on tonight?"

The officer shook his head. "You can take him to the game, but if he gets a bullet in the head, it's not my fault," the officer said as he turned and walked back toward his car.

Eli looked over to Sam as he drove to the jail. "Buddy, we have a problem. Even the cops are fearful for Jamaal's life. What do we do with this?"

Sam's answer was quick and to the point. "Jamaal is an adult. We go to the jail and tell him about the threat. Then we do nothing. He has to decide what risk he is willing to take."

Sam simply said, "Let's get to the jail, inform Jamaal about what has been told to us, and let him make the choice as far as what he is going to do."

Twenty-five minutes later, Eli and Sam arrived at the LA county jail. They walked in. The desk sergeant sent for Jamaal. The three of them were escorted to a conference room to talk. Sam and Eli were seated on one side of the table, Jamaal on the other.

Eli began, "Jamaal, I know this is not something we have done before, but I was stopped on the freeway today by an officer, who gave me a piece of information that bothered both Sam and I. The guys you put away have put a hit on you. The officials are worried about your safety. The drug lords are not getting out of jail and don't want you to enjoy your life on the outside when your term here is over. They understand the pros are watching your performance, and they want to make sure you don't get to the pros."

⚾ ⚾ ⚾

Pete looked over at Father and asked, "Father, can you protect Jamaal from those guys who want to hurt him?"

The Father answered instantly, "Pete, I have been using Jamaal to reach those I bring him in contact within the jail. I know the time everyone is born and when they are going to die. These guys won't hurt Jamaal. His time is short, but not yet."

Peter's look of questioning would surprise anyone, except Father, as he asked, "What do you mean his time is short?"

The Father responded vaguely, "Pete, people's choices have consequences."

Jamaal looked at the two guys and simply said, "The Word says 'Perfect love cast out all fear,' Christ has given me perfect love. David did not walk in fear when everything went against him. Joseph walked in God's favor even when everything looked as though he had lost. Paul said, 'To live is Christ, to die is gain.' There are lessons that can be gained if God allows me to live. And there are lessons to be learned if I am taken out of here early. I gain either way. I remember years back, watching TV in the lounge. Bristol Palin was on *Dancing with the Stars*. They were receiving all kinds of negative response. She simply said, 'Let's just dance.' I am going to walk with Christ until the day he calls me home. Let's play ball."

Eli and Sam looked at each other. Eli smiled. "Let's play ball." He got up as the other two did, and they walked out of the room. They got to the door, and Sam turned to Jamaal.

"Man, they said no practice. Just sit tight. They are expecting you at practice today. That won't happen, but we did speak to the authorities, and we will practice Tuesday this week instead. You will play in the game."

Tuesday came. They picked up Jamaal at the jail and took him to practice.

Eli looked over at Sam and said, "Buddy, you and I both know that we can also get Jamaal out to speak to the kids. We have been working on our music a lot. I think we are ready for a concert."

Sam got a curious look on his face, as he said, "What is it you have in mind, friend?"

Eli gave a quick answer. "Look, we have our final game of the season on Wednesday. We then have one playoff game on Friday. It's our last game, so let's have a concert. We do warm up then have the YFC band really rock the crowd." Eli looked at Jamaal in the rearview mirror and continued, "Then in the middle of the whole thing, we have you give your testimony about what you have done and how drugs kill kids."

Sam got a huge smile on his face as he said, "That just might work."

Arriving at the field, Eli looked at Jamaal. "Today, you're gonna get in the batter's box and not get out until you hit me."

Jamaal got a look on his face that said, "This is gonna be a long practice."

Getting out of the SUV, they unlocked the cuffs. Jamaal went into the warm-up shack to change clothes. Eli walked over to Sam and said, "Buddy, he will probably hit me pretty quickly. I haven't thrown in years 'cause of the shoulder. Wonder what I still have."

Eli walked and prayed. "Father, just let me have some of the stuff you used to give me. This guy has to be able to hit me in order to make the pros. I really feel that you are going to use him in your purpose."

🏐 🏐 🏐

The Father looked over at Peter. "Eli still has the gift. His shoulder could not take much of the speed he can put on the ball, but he will find out in short order I don't take away the gifts I give people. They lose use of them when they do not use them, but the gifts are there."

Thumbnail asked Father, "May I play on his shoulder like I used to when he was pitching?"

With a smile as broad as the ocean, the Father said, "Have at it, little one. Have some fun."

Eli walked to the mound. Jamaal was standing in the batter's box. Suddenly he heard a familiar voice. Thumbnail said to him, "Hey buddy, I'm back!"

Eli heard the drums, the driving drums. "Secret Ambition" started playing through his mind. He realized what this was still all about: the kids. Jamaal had to reach the kids. This whole thing is for the concert being set up to draw the kids, and the kids will come, and they will hear the Word of Christ's love. He looked down at Jamaal, tossed the ball in the air, and smoked one in at 105! Jamaal was not even close. Eli smiled.

Thumbnail said, "You still have it, buddy. Keep throwing those strikes."

Eli threw fifteen strikes in a row. Jamaal was starting to get really frustrated.

"How can I hit you? No one could hit you in the majors. How do you expect me to hit you?"

Thumbnail started telling Eli how to respond. "It's a matter of timing. My pitches are coming fast. Think about it, with a normal pitcher, where you start to swing. You must speed up your swing just a fraction to get a piece of what I am throwing. When you do that, the ball will be outta here."

Eli walked back to the mound and threw another fast ball, and Jamaal tipped it foul, then another pitch and another foul.

Thumbnail said, "Give him a change up." Eli did, and Jamaal swung a second early and spun around. The grin and chuckle of Eli really ticked off Jamaal. Eli, smiling, settled down.

Eli threw another fast ball. Jamaal drove it out of the park, smiling, as he ran the bases.

Eli sent him out to the field to take some fielding practice and gave the ball to some of the other pitchers. As Eli rotated his shoulder, he realized the soreness that was there from the pitches that he had thrown.

Practice was over, so it was back to jail for Jamaal. Jamaal walked in, and the officer removed the cuffs. Jamaal was escorted back to his cell. As he arrived back at his cell, he could see a person there that was new to the jail. Tattoos of skulls and crossbones, satanic images, witches, and every kind of evil known to man were tattooed on his body.

Jamaal walked over to him and extended his hand in friendship. The inmate looked the other way and walked to his corner of the cell.

Jamaal said, "Hey man, what's up? We are stuck with each other. At least we can be civil."

Lawrence, the new cellmate, simply said, "You wanna die, keep pushin' in on me."

Thumbnail jumped over to Lawrence. "Back off on him, mister! Jamaal knows God! You mess with him, you mess with God!"

Lawrence looked around himself, "Who said dat?"

Jamaal smiled. He had heard that little voice for years now. He understood that it must have been a servant of the Most High. Jamaal just smiled to himself.

Lawrence lay in his bunk, looked up at the ceiling, and Thumbnail started talking a mile a minute. "Listen, dude, you may think you're tough, but God Almighty, who sent his Son, Jesus, to pay the price so you could be cleansed, wants to talk to you. Ask Jamaal how you can hear his voice."

Lawrence shook his head again, rolled over, and tried to sleep. Thumbnail kept saying the same thing over and over. Finally Lawrence shouted, "Shut up! Just shut up!"

Jamaal just laid back in his bunk, trying hard to keep from busting out in huge laughter.

"What's wrong, man, hearing voices?" Jamaal asked, grinning to himself.

Again, he heard the words, "Shut up! Just SHUT UP!"

Thumbnail spoke up again, "What's wrong? Can't understand who's talkin' to ya?" as he giggled, in a way that only Lawrence could hear.

"SHUT UP!" Lawrence shouted.

"God's not going give up on you, dude. Better start asking Jamaal how to get saved," Thumbnail said.

○ ○ ○

Pete looked over at the Father. "Father, this is driving Lawrence nuts. How long are you going to let Thumbnail keep it up?"

Father chuckled as he answered, "Until he listens. I have plans for that young man."

⚾ ⚾ ⚾

That night, the angel, Gabriel, was sent to Lawrence in a dream. He entered into the sleep of Lawrence.

Gabriel said, "Lawrence, it's time to stop running. God wants to use you. You can either submit to His will or things are going to continue on the path where you are heading. Your body will be dead, and your spirit will be afflicted for eternity. Talk to Jamaal. He can show you how to hear the voice of the great I Am."

⚾ ⚾ ⚾

Jamaal was lying on his bunk, and he heard Lawrence tossing and turning. Suddenly, he sat straight up in bed, looked over at Jamaal, and yelled, "Okay, dude, how do I get saved? I can't take hearing these voices. And even in my dreams they are driving me nuts."

Jamaal sat up on his bunk and said, "Look, buddy, it's time to stop running from God, receive Christ as your Lord and Savior, and it's time to start running to Him."

The two men prayed together for the first time. The next day, Lawrence would be released. He would walk out a free man. Jamaal would not taste that freedom for another six months.

The next morning, Jamaal was sleeping extremely soundly. Suddenly, the guard shouted, "Jamaal! Get out of bed! There is someone here to see ya!"

"Who? What?" was all that Jamaal could say as he dragged himself out of the bunk. The pastor, Brad Johnson, of the First Church was standing there. "Yes, sir! What can I do for you?" Jamaal said with total respect.

"Jamaal, you have a great number of kids looking up to you. They need to know what you have done and why you're here. Part of your sentence, as you may recall, is to share with kids so they will realize the danger that drugs and the scum who sell them are to their well-being. They also need to know, even more than the danger that drugs pose, the power that Christ has to change lives. We are having a huge rally tonight. I have arranged for you to speak."

The quizzical look on Jamaal's face was quite telling of his emotions about this whole thing. "Where am I speaking?" he asked.

The answer that came ever so quickly put a look of fear on Jamaal's face. "There is a Youth for Christ meeting tonight. Many of the kids who are going to be there were just released from a juvenile detention center. They are who you were ten years ago."

Jamaal shook his head. Thumbnail told him, "Jamaal buddy, don't worry. I will make sure you have all the right words to tell those young men. They will be on their faces before the Most High God, repenting of their sins."

Jamaal looked around, trying once again to figure out who was talking to him. "Who said that?" were the words that came out of his mouth before he had a chance to stop them.

Jamaal sat in his cell for hours, trying to figure out just what he was going to say that night at the Youth for Christ rally. The words wouldn't come. He wrote, threw the papers in the waste basket, wrote some more, threw the papers in the basket. This went on all afternoon. Finally, it was 6:00 p.m. The guard came to his cell.

"Jamaal, it's time. Eli is here for ya. Let's get the jewelry on," the guard told him.

Jamaal thought to himself, *It's time. Isn't that what they say to a guy as he walks to the execution chamber?* Little did he know of the life that his words would bring to the ones attending the rally.

The Father looked over at Pete. "Now you're going to see me work."

Pete answered, "What are you going to do, Father?"

To which the Father responded, "Jamaal's chains and the chains of many there tonight will fall off, and they will walk in freedom."

Jamaal heard the conversation between the Father and Peter. He thought to himself.

"Those chains fell off a long time ago when Christ walked into my life. That's when my true freedom started."

The three of them climbed into the BMW SUV and headed for the rally.

Eli reached up, put on his sunglasses to block the rays of the hot California sun. He looked in his rearview mirror and said to Jamaal, "You know what you're going to say, buddy?"

Jamaal had a very worried look on his face. "Not a clue, Eli. I have been working on this all day, and then I hear this little voice tell me not to worry about it. When the words are needed, they will be there. Kind of like in the Bible where it says when they haul you into court, not to worry about what you will say. So I guess I am not going to worry about it."

Just then he heard Thumbnail. "Jamaal, with me, you will be great." Then Thumbnail heard Father speaking, "With whom, Thumbnail?"

Thumbnail responded, "With you, Father."

The Father replied, "Let's not forget that little bit of truth."

Jamaal looked around the car. He heard both voices. "Am I going crazy?" he asked.

As they arrived at the Youth for Christ Center, Jamaal stuck his head out the door and vomited green yuck all over, looked up, and said, "Let's go!"

The Youth for Christ (YFC) band was playing some real loud Christian rock. Jamaal's eyes lit up when he heard the music. Suddenly, the music stopped. The place got real quiet. Matthew Shepard, the head of YFC in Los Angeles, called Jamaal to the podium. "Young people here tonight, we have a special treat for you. To speak with us tonight is Jamaal Johnson, someone who Christ has changed forever."

Jamaal walked to the podium with confidence. As he pulled out his papers, he heard Thumbnail. "Put the papers down. I will tell you what to say. Truth will be spoken here tonight."

Jamaal put his papers on the table beside his podium. He looked at the room filled with young people. He started simply. "Tonight is going to change some of your lives. Tonight, some of you are going to meet the same Christ you have thought you have known for years.

"When I was younger, I thought selling drugs was a cool thing. I thought it was a way of making some serious money. Then one day, I sold drugs to a ten-year-old boy. He had red hair, big brown eyes, always smiling, a totally innocent, happy-go-lucky kid. I took his last two dollars and watched him die when he took the meth. I saw a happy ten-year-old convulse, puke, and die. I did it to him. I took his innocence for two bucks. And I watched him die." Thumbnail had a tear running down his cheek.

Peter looked over at The Father as The Father raised the little red-haired boy to sit on his lap.

"Father, why did that man sell me that poison?" the little red-headed boy asked The Father. "Father, I like it here and all, but I know my mom misses me dearly, and I hurt because I know she hurts. Why did he do it? Why did he hurt so many people?"

The Most High God looked lovingly at the little red-headed boy sitting on his lap.

"It's like this. Your heart was pure and innocent. I had touched your heart the moment you were born. I touched his as well, but for a person to love me, to really love me, they must have the choice not to love me. For a while he chose not to love me, until he met Eli and his wife Jill. Before he met them he had already sold you the poison. He went to jail for that, but I was able to touch his heart because of Eli. I used Eli and Sam to reach him. I also used him to get a lot of very evil men off the street so they won't hurt other kids."

Then the great I Am took the little red-headed boy by the hand, and they walked down streets that shone so bright it almost made one's eyes hurt. He looked at the little boy and said, "Your life on earth was short, but I used it. I brought great joy to your mommy and daddy. I am giving them another little girl who will be a great servant of mine. Your mom will always miss you. There will always be a hole in her heart just your size."

The little red-haired boy looked at the Father, squeezed his hand, and asked, "So my death saved a lot of other little boys and girls?"

Father picked the little boy up and gave him a huge hug. "It did, and the man who gave you the poison is now serving me, but…"

The little red-haired boy got a quizzical look on his face. "But what?" he questioned The Father.

The Father, in his loving voice, told the little red-headed boy, "When the time is right, you will find out."

Jamaal finished his story about selling drugs. He explained to the young people in attendance what a bad guy he had been. He also took the time to also explain what Christ did in his life. Thumbnail was in tears. He knew the little red-headed boy was with the Father.

Jamaal gave an invitation for people to receive Christ as their Lord and Savior, and the kids ran to the podium. Jamaal, Eli, and Sam spent the next three hours praying for the kids.

At the end, it was time for Eli to take Jamaal back to the jail. The kids saw them put the cuffs on Jamaal. One of the older boys asked, "What are the cuffs for?"

Jamaal, with a tear in his eye, said, "I am still serving time for the crime I committed. I also have to live with what I did to that little red-headed boy for the rest of my life. Do me a favor, kid, keep your heart pure and your mind on Christ. You'll be okay." Jamaal got in the back of the BMW SUV and headed back to the jail.

The young men looked at each other; bewilderment was on each of their faces as the band started to play. Sam walked to the microphone. "Young men and women, what you have seen here is a broken man. He plays a great game of baseball, but the pain he caused a mom, the life he took from the little boy, can never be repaid. Jamaal can work the rest of his life trying to accomplish good, yet the only way he will be able to really live with himself is to live a life that is totally Christ-centered. It's only by coming to a complete faith in Christ that he can find redemption," Sam said.

Carl Simpson, one of the teenagers in the group asked a question. The dark light of the room with the spotlight on the stage put almost an angelic glow on the face of the young man as he asked, "If he can't do anything in this life to redeem himself, what can be done to make his life worth living?"

◦ ◦ ◦

The Father looked over at Peter and said, "This is where the rubber really meets the road. This is where I have one scripture that will show these young people. If they truly trust me and they really let my calling be on their life, then I can work even the most evil thing for their good."

"Father, how can you take an evil, like what happened to the little red-headed boy, and make it good?" Peter asked.

A tear came to the Father's eye as he said, "I did not say in my Word that I make evil good. What I said is I will work something good from it. The birth of the little red-headed boy's sister is a good I brought out of his senseless death."

◦ ◦ ◦

Sam looked directly at Carl and said, "God, in His Word, said, 'All things work together for good, for those who love God, and are called according to his purpose.' What we have to remember is that somehow, someway, God will make good come out of the evil that is delivered to us. We just have to be looking for it."

Simpson got a look of disgust on his face. "How could a loving God make something good come out of such an evil thing?"

Sam turned to the janitor and asked him to turn up the lights. He saw Simpson with the same look on his face of disgust. Sam asked the question. "Carl, how did you come to Christ?" He knew the answer to the question before he even asked it.

The answer raised eyebrows with the whole group.

"I was in jail for a DWI, and Jamaal led me to Christ. I stopped running from God and allowed Him to touch my heart,"

Sam asked one more question. "Do you think it's good that God saved you?"

"Of course" was the answer from Simpson.

Thumbnail was getting tired because of the energy the little angel was using as he kept feeding the answers to Sam.

Simpson's eyes started to get really teary. The weeping that followed soon became uncontrollable. The crying of this broken man came from deep within, so far deep within his whole body that he started to shake with the emotion when he understood the price that was paid so he could be cleansed of his sin, and to be made Holy, and walk in the newness that only Christ would give.

The Father had the little red-headed boy sitting on his lap. The boy was crying as hard as Simpson. Then Christ got up from his thrown and walked over to the red-headed boy, tears running down as he looked at the little boy and said, "I really love you. Your family hurts, and they miss you. Nothing can be done to help that hurt right now, but my love will sustain them through all of this. I can take the all evil things and make something positive and good come out of it."

The little red-headed boy looked at the Father and asked one simple question. "Does my mom still know that I love her?"

The Father called Thumbnail and asked him one question. "Thumbnail, what have I had you telling the little red-headed boy's mom just before she goes to sleep every night?"

Thumbnail jumped on the little red-headed boy's nose, looked him in the eye, and told him. "Every night I tell your mom that you really, really love her. And then I tell her that someday she is going to see you again."

The grin on the little red-headed boy lit up heaven, and the joy of knowing that he will see his mom again warmed his little heart.

Just then, the little red-headed boy looked over at Gabriel and saw a cute little girl peeking around his robe as she was standing behind him. She smiled, and heaven lit up. The little red-headed boy asked the Father, "Who is that?"

The Father chuckled a bit. "I want to introduce you to Hannah. She is a little girl that was never born. Her mommy and daddy loved her a lot even before she was born, but she was not to be."

The little red-headed boy asked, "Father, why?"

The Father smiled. "Sometimes it is better not having some questions answered," was the answer the Father gave in a loving and caring way.

Hannah ran up to the little red-headed boy and said, "C'mon, we have a lot to explore. It's time to go swim with the dolphins, then we will ride the elephants."

The little red-headed boy jumped down off of the Fathers lap, a huge smile on his face, and ran off with Eli and Jill's daughter to explore heaven with her.

Simpson had been allowed to see everything that went on in heaven as the band played. He shook his head in disbelief. He asked himself, *What did I just see? What is going on here?"* as the tears just kept pouring down his cheeks.

Thumbnail jumped on Simpson's shoulder. "Carl, it's like this, you have just seen the little boy that Jamaal killed. You have seen the love and caring of The Father and the Son for this little boy. Now it's time for you to walk out the journey that Father has for you. It's time for you to let the Father touch your spirit with His. It's time for your oneness with the Father to be complete."

Simpson shook his head and asked himself, "How do I do that? How do I become one with God?"

Thumbnail had the answer, "Through Jesus the Christ, his death, and resurrection."

15
The Big Game

PETER WALKED UP to the Father and ruffled the hair of the little red-headed boy and said, "Father, we are getting really close to the time when Herman starts to come into his own as a ball player. Through all of these years, Eli has been making sure he paid attention to little Herman's ball playing, but what are you going to do with him?"

The Father got a grin on his face. "First, we have to get Jamaal through the next three months of his sentence. Then we will launch the great Herman McBrien."

● ● ●

It was Sunday morning. Eli, Jill, and Herm had attended Mass the night before where Herm was totally caught up in the majesty of the mass; ten-year-old Herman came running into Jill and Eli's room and jumped on the bed. "Come on, Mom and Dad, we have to get headed to church."

Eli rolled over and simply said, "Go away."

Jill got up, walked over, hugged little Herman, and said, "C'mon, champ. Mommy loves you. Do you remember what the priest talked about last night in his sermon?"

Herman with his great smile answered correctly, "Yup! He talked about the gifts we are given by our Father in heaven and how we have to use them to be the part of God's purpose here on earth."

Thumbnail jumped on Eli's forehead. "Listen, mister, that's your son who wants to go worship your Heavenly Father for the second time in two days. He has a love for the Father that must be fed. Get your butt out of bed, NOW!"

Eli had heard that little voice many times in many ways and knew he better listen.

Eli simply asked, "Why, why can't I sleep in ever?"

Thumbnail, standing on his nose, simply said, "A little sleep, a little slumber leads to destruction. If not yours, then your son's. Do you want that?"

Eli knew his son had something special with the Christ, and he knew he had to work to develop that relationship.

Eli shook his head, got up, and headed downstairs and grabbed his ten-year-old son. He started rubbing his knuckles into his head and said, "Herm, you gonna win today?"

Herm struggled out of his dad's embrace. "You know it, Dad, but first we proclaim the victory in worship. I am the fastest on the team, and today, if the situation is right, the coach wants me to steal bases." Eli looked over at Jill, smiled, and kissed those lips that were reserved for him and said. "Let's go! We have a game to get to right after worship."

Jill and Eli hit the shower and then came downstairs. Herman was standing by the picture window. The bright California sun was shining in, casting a shadow of Herman across the carpet. Herman was watching his shadow as he swung. He was trying to make sure his form was perfect.

The Father looked over at Peter and said, "Look at Herman. He is already looking at his own minute actions in order to become the best hitter he can possibly be. This trait is going to serve him well as a pro."

Peter looked over toward the brightness that is the Father and said, "Father, you're amazing! You designed the most powerful computer ever and put it inside man's head. Because of that, Herman was able to analyze his swing via a shadow."

Father chuckled. "Just watch this kid of mine. You think I did great things with his dad, you have not seen anything yet. Pete, remember, a parent's sin is passed to the second and third generation, so is a parent's greatness."

Eli, Jill, and Herman walked into the service at First Church. The music was just about to start; then Pastor Johnson would be preaching on the man with the talents. His words were not those condemning the man who did not use his talents but words that were a rally cry for the body to start using the talents they had been given for the furtherance of our Father's kingdom.

Herman, having gotten really excited with the music, started to really get excited with the pastor's teaching. He leaned into Eli and simply said, "Dad, I am gonna use the talent that The Father has given me. I am gonna be a great baseball player. But how can the Father use a base-ball player?"

Eli simply said, "We will talk about it after the service. Please, we need to hear Pastor Johnson."

When the last song was sung, the last prayer prayed, Herman jumped up from his chair and sprinted for the car. He swung open the door, grabbed his uniform, and made a mad dash for the church restroom. Two minutes later, he flew out and ran down the steps. Jill grabbed him and said, "Hold it there, buddy, where are the clothes you changed out of?"

Herman got a sheepish look on his face. "Oh yeah! I almost forgot my clothes." He turned around and made another mad dash back to the men's room, grabbed his clothes, and ran full tilt for the car. Once in the car with his mom and dad, they headed for the ball park. His excitement was enough to bounce the car as they cruised down the Interstate toward the ball park. Arriving at the park, Herman jumped out of the car, grabbed his baseball glove off the car floor, and sprung over to where his team was gathered. The coach, Mike Schmidt, started to hit infield practice. Herman, playing second base, was able to snatch balls out of the air and then burn them home with light-ning speed. Kevin Derusha, the shortstop, looked over at

Herman and asked him, "Why aren't you pitching, with an arm like that?"

Herman shrugged his shoulders and responded, "Not my thing. I would rather field and burn the ball back to the catcher," Herman said as he walked around the diamond with his chest puffed up.

Peter looked over at The Father. "Are you going to let his pride show like that? Shouldn't he be showing his humbleness in all that he does?"

Father chuckled slightly and said, "Pete, it's like this, Herman is pretty young at his point in his life. I let him strut his stuff. I will have his dad and mom reign in his pride. They have a way of teaching him that pride really does come before the fall. If he refuses to listen to mom and dad, then as you well know, I do have my ways."

Herman, at ten years old, walked up to bat. All the kids are standing there, cheering him on. Eli and Jill were leaning over the fence and praying their little boy would make a show for himself.

Father looked over at Peter and said, "Pete, he is about to experience his first homerun. Watch how he reacts."

Pete shook his head, "Father, how is a huge success at this point, going to help him?"

The Father simply said, "Peter, when are you going to learn to trust that I really do have a plan?"

Peter got a sheepish look on his face as he said, "Father, I know you know what's best, I really do. Sometimes, even I try to think three steps ahead of where you're going and what you're doing. I guess I will always get to learn something new."

⚾ ⚾ ⚾

Herman was staring at the pitcher. He took an old trick from his dad and winked. The pitcher started to get a frazzled look on his face. The pitcher wound up and let the ball fly. Herman swung perfectly and hard. He got a piece of the ball and drove it out of the ball park. As he rounded the bases, his hands raised in triumph, pointed to his own chest, and tripped and fell on his face. He got up, looked over at Eli, who simply pointed to heaven and smiled. Herman looked up to heaven, felt the warmth of Father's smile, and pointed to heaven and finished running the bases for his first home run.

⚾ ⚾ ⚾

Pete looked over at The Father and simply said, "It's going to be subtle reminders from Eli, I take it? You will always get the credit."

The Father just sat on his huge golden throne with the Christ at his right hand and smiled at Peter. He did not need to say a word.

◊ ◊ ◊

Herman walked into the dugout as his coach gave him high five. Herman's smile lit up the dugout almost as much as his sister's, Hannah's, smile lit up heaven. Three more times during the game, Herman would come up to bat, and three times he would strike out. After the game, on his way home, his dad, looking in the rearview mirror at his son, simply asked one question, "Were you trying to hit a home run for you, or were you trying to help your team?"

Herman got a downtrodden look on his face. "Honestly, Dad, I was trying to bring glory to myself."

Eli reached over, took Jill's hand, and squeezed it. They both knew that their son would learn a very important lesson from this.

Eli then said to Herman, "Son, it's like this, when we work out of motives that are pure, when we work out of motives to help others and don't worry about ourselves, then Father can bless us in what we are doing. When we do things to bring glory to ourselves, then we are on our own. Father won't bless our efforts when they are to bring glory to ourselves. Remember, we are to lay up for ourselves rewards in heaven."

Little Herman looked at his dad and asked a very simple question. "Dad, what kind of rewards do we get in heaven?

This question hit Eli like a ton of bricks. He had no idea how to answer. He looked over at his sweet bride. She gave him a look that said, "You're on your own on this one, better start praying.

Suddenly Eli had a bolt of lightning hit him that would direct Herman to the answer of his question. "Bud, there are two things you can do to dig up the answer to that question. One is to grab the concordance when you get home, the other is to ask Pastor Johnson and Father Michael the next time you see them."

Herman then asked a follow-up question that left Eli speechless. "Dad, you have no idea, do you?"

Herman could see Eli's sheepish grin as he drove. "No, son, I have no idea. We will have to research this together."

⚾ ⚾ ⚾

The Father looked over at Peter and said," Pete, I am about to have little Herman ask his dad another question that is going to be on his mind all night. But I will give him the answer he needs to satisfy his son."

⚾ ⚾ ⚾

With a glint and a sparkle in his eye, Herman asked Eli, "Dad, you played baseball, right?"

Eli looked over at Jill as to say silently, *What's he going to ask now?* Then he answered, "Yup, sure did."

"And they paid you *a lot* of money, right?"

Jill grinned and flashed a smile and said with her eyes, "Get yourself out of this one, buddy."

"And you have a lot left, right?" Herman asked, with a sly grin on his face.

"Yup" was the quick answer.

"Then what kinda reward will you have in heaven?" came the question, that would be on Eli's mind for the rest of the night.

The Father got a mischievous grin on his face. "Now watch, Peter, how I have Thumbnail whisper the answer to Jill."

Jill spoke up and gave the answer that satisfied Herman. "Champ, our Father chooses to bless those who are willing to use the wealth that He gives them when they seek His face on building His kingdom. Jesus always guided your dad on where he was to invest the money. Our Heavenly Father gave him wealth to be the most effective in helping kids to really know God's love through Christ. For instance, your dad helped start the Masters Construction Company that we run now, building hospitals, churches, homes, and rebuilding the ghettos. And we hire as many people from the ghetto as we can."

Herman looked at his mom and dad and thought to himself, *my dad is a great man!*

Having been riding the elephants and swimming with the dolphins for the better part of a day, the little red-headed boy and Hannah came running up to Father.

The little red-headed boy asked Father, "Father, we would like to see what is going on with our moms and dads. Is that possible?"

With that, the Father opened up the window of heaven, and they were able to see what was going on with their moms and dads. Hannah looked at little Herman, riding with his mom and dad in the back seat. "Is that my brother?" she asked the Father.

Father smiled at her as he said, "Yes, sweetheart, it is. His name is Herman. It will be eighty years before he gets to meet you, but he will know you the second he walks through the gates."

The little red-headed boy asked, "Will my little sister know me?"

Father gave a great big hug, smiled, and simply said, "Yup."

      ⚾   ⚾   ⚾

Sunday was coming to an end. The sun was starting to set, and Eli and Jill were sitting on the balcony overlooking the ocean and watching the sun set over the Pacific. Eli reached over and took Jill's hand and simply asked, "That question that Herman asked me today is still on my mind. Hun, do you think I am handling the money the way Father wants me to?"

Thumbnail jumped on Jill's shoulder right next to her ear and said, "Tell him that Father gave him the wealth because he knew from the time he was a child that his desire would always be to serve the Master with the Master's money. Remember, in the Word we are told 'To him who much is given, much is required.'"

Jill smiled and repeated what Thumbnail had just told her. Eli looked at his bride. The sunlight on her face gave her the appearance of an angel. Then she finished with her own thoughts, "Hun, what attracted me to you in the first place was not the fact that you were the greatest baseball player that our high school had ever seen, although that did not hurt. What attracted me to you was, when we looked at each other in the gym for the first time, I could see the Holy Spirit all over you. Eli, your secret ambition that we talked about so much was to see the Spirit of Christ touching kids in a powerful way. If it were not for you, Jamaal would be in jail for the rest of his life. And the kids he had been able to reach, because of your working with him to become a good baseball player, would not have been reached. Eli, the question that Herman asked of you was for the purpose of knowing that you have been, and are, using the wealth that has been given to you to build His kingdom as it should be used."

Hannah, having been allowed to see what just went on, said to the Father, "My mom and dad are pretty cool folks, and I can see my little brother is full of questions. What is he going to be when he grows up, Father?" she asked sweetly.

The great I Am smiled at the little girl he created. He touched her cheek as only a kind, loving Father could. The Father looked into her sweet eyes and simply said, "So you want me to give you a glimpse into the future, do you?"

Hannah smiled with that smile he created in her, much like the one he gave Jill, totally disarming. Father smiled and simply said, "Let me just tell you this, he is destined for greatness." As He smiled even more warmly and gently, He touched the bottom of Hannah's chin, lifting it so she would look directly into his eyes, which brought warmth to Hannah's whole being.

After Jill's supportive comments, Eli was able to relax and enjoy the rest of the evening, at least until the phone rang. Jill got up, grabbed Eli's cell, and tossed it to him, smiling.

Eli looked at his phone and saw that it was Aaron calling. "What's up, dude? Talk to me."

Aaron gave a short, quick answer, "We have been challenged to a game by UCIA. Their coach said there is no way a 'church league' team could beat them. It seems that Jamaal had been shooting his mouth off. What do we do now?"

Eli had only one thing to say. "Play ball! Call the coach and set up the game." They both said good-bye, and Aaron made the calls to get the game set up.

Twenty minutes later, Aaron called back with the news and said to Eli, "It is set, Friday night at the UIA Stadium."

Eli simply stated, "I want you calling everyone on the team. I will get a hold of Jamaal. We start tomorrow night with practice for the next three nights and a team meeting on Thursday night and the game on Friday. One other thing, bro. Jamaal will like all this time outside his cell. We have got to do it right, or we get our butts kicked, and personally, I don't care for that thought."

◌ ◌ ◌

The team practiced hard. They did not let up for a second. Eli worked with his pitchers, showing them how to increase the speed on every pitch. He worked them in such a way that he would be able to get three hard innings out of each of the men he would have on the mound.

All the time he spent with his pitchers, he had heard the drums, the beat, the guitars, and keyboards playing "Secret Ambition" in his mind. As he heard the sounds in his mind, he realized he was living it out.

Sam had been spending the week working with the hitters, teaching them what to look for in the pitchers and how to tell what pitches they were going to throw. He had Eli throwing pitches at speeds that no one could hit so they would be able to get their bats around quick enough to get a hold of the pitches that UCIA would be throwing at them.

Finally, Friday arrived, and the team was a bundle of nerves. Players were throwing up in the locker room. They looked at the clock, and it was game time. Eli stepped forward, "Okay, men, lets pray." Everyone dropped to their knees while Eli led them in a prayer. "Father, you took David to victories he should not have won. Gideon won a huge battle with only a few totally committed soldiers.

Father, the men from the UCIA team want to humiliate the Christian men playing here. They don't believe these men have really been changed by you. Father, normally I would not ask for a victory, and I won't tonight. I just ask you to glorify yourself on that field tonight: In Jesus' name, Amen."

◊ ◊ ◊

Peter looked over at the great I Am and simply asked, "Are you going to answer that prayer today, Father?"

With a sly grin on his face, Father simply said four short but very meaningful words, "You know it, Peter."

◊ ◊ ◊

Eli led his team into the stadium with fifty thousand screaming fans. He looked back to make sure his team was really following him out. Jamaal was leading the team out. He looked up in the stands and saw the little red-headed boy's mom. She was making her way to the dugout. The security people were going to try to stop her. Jamaal said to Eli, "Have them let her through. I just really feel this is going to be okay."

The little red-headed boy's mom walked up to Jamaal and said, "I still hate you for what you did to my son, but now I know the testimony you gave at the trial of the kingpins saved a great many little boys and girls. So at least I don't feel like he died in vain. I forgive you." She turned and walked away before Jamaal could say anything.

The announcer sounded like someone out of the second century. "Ladies and Gentlemen! Today you will get to see the Christians from First Church learn a valuable lesson. That not even God can make this team good enough to beat the National Champion Lions of UCIA."

Father looked over at Peter. The fire in his eyes gave away the anger he felt toward the announcer for his lack of respect for the great I Am. The Father, in his anger over what they were predicting would happen to this ball club, said, "Peter, I am going to see that this is one time when they try to feed my people to the lions, and the lions will be totally destroyed."

Rick James was the first pitcher to take the mound. As he got ready to leave the dugout and all the players were around Eli, Eli spoke these words. "Not by might, not by power, but by my Spirit says the Lord. Gentlemen, it's time to become instruments of warfare. When I was in high school, a batter made a ridiculing statement about God's power, and I said these words and threw one of the fastest balls I had ever thrown. It's time to let the spirit take control of your whole being. It's time to really show these people the power that our Heavenly Father does have." With that, Eli sent the team out onto the field.

James walked to the mound. He heard the music, and he looked around himself, trying to figure out where it's coming from. He shrugged and went into his wind up. He threw a ball that came out of his hand so fast he could not believe it. He threw pitch after pitch, and no one could hit him. Three outs and First Church was up to bat.

The first batter got walked, the second got a single, and the third got a single. Jamaal walked up to the plate. Thumbnail was sitting on his shoulder and said, "Jamaal, point to the left field fence!"

Peter started to get excited at this display of pride that Thumbnail was trying to get Jamaal to do. He looked to Father and asked, "Father, should Thumbnail be promoting pride in one's own ability this way?"

Father responded, "This is not promoting his pride, but he will give me the credit for what is about to happen."

Peter smiled and nodded.

Jamaal shook his head and pointed to the left field fence, reminiscent of Babe Ruth. The pitcher for UCIA went into his wind up and threw a fastball. Jamaal swung, and the ball was gone, over the left field fence. Thumbnail, riding on his shoulder, simply said to him, "Point to the One who gave you this hit." Jamaal raised his arm, looks up to heaven, smiled, and pointed as he rounded the bases.

The Father looked at Peter. "I told you I would get the credit for this one," he said as he smiled.

0   0   0

With a four-run lead, that would turn into a twelve-to-nothing route for UCIA. The men on the First Church team were feeling an excitement that could only come with a victory that was ordained by God the Father himself. As the game ended, the manager for the UCIA team walked over to Eli, took hold of his hand, and said to him, "How did you ever put together a team of this caliber of deadbeats from the ghetto?"

Eli shook his hand and said, "You have just witnessed the power of God Almighty, through his Son, Jesus the Christ, by the Holy Spirit. You would be wise to go home and ponder what happened here today. As David said to Goliath, 'Not by might, not by power, but by my Spirit says the Lord.'" With that, Eli smiled and trotted back to his team.

Before he could get to the team, Henderson, LA's manager, caught up to Eli. He put his arm around Eli's shoulder and said to him, "That Jamaal on your team, he's pretty good! When is his jail time done?"

Eli first said, "You do understand you can't talk to him until he is out of jail, don't you?" Henderson stepped aside as the sun was shining into his eyes, and he nodded in the affirmative. He then asked again, "How long?"

Squinting in the sun, Eli responded, "Three months."

Henderson responded, "After this game, he should be a big draw," and turned and walked away.

Eli walked to the team and immediately was asked one question. "Was that Henderson, your old manager?"

Eli stooped down, pulled pieces of grass, and asked Father what he should tell them. He asked the Father, through the Son, just what he should tell Jamaal.

The Father yelled at Thumbnail, "It's time to quit playing with the kids and start to get back to work. In his heart, my Holy Spirit is telling Eli what he should be saying right now. Thumbnail, he needs to hear the words. I want you to be telling him exactly what to say to Jamaal."

Eli walked over to the team. He answered the question with the smoothness of a salesman with years and years of experience. "Yup, he did have something special to ask me, but at this time, I am not at liberty to say what it was." He then grabbed the cuffs and put them on Jamaal, and they headed for the car to be able to get Jamaal back to jail. As they started the long drive back to the jail, Eli simply said, "Jamaal, Henderson has a job for you with the team when you're done with your jail term in three months."

Jamaal got a quizzical look on his face and asked, "What kind of job?"

Thumbnail whispered to Eli, "Tell him it is something he will enjoy doing, but not to get too excited about it."

Elli shrugged, "It's something you will enjoy. Just don't get too excited about it. But that the condition of your probation must be met."

⚾ ⚾ ⚾

The Father called Thumbnail into His presence and said to him, "Good job, little one! You listen well to the instructions of my Spirit. You will be useful to me for generations to come."

Thumbnail could only smile at the Father. The joy he felt, knowing that the Father was proud of him, boiled over into a jig. And boy, could that little angel dance the jig!

*   *   *

As Eli and Jamaal walked into the jail, Eli could see the tears starting to flow down Jamaal's cheeks as he walked toward his cell. "What is it man?" Eli asked him as they walked into the brightly lit receiving area of the jail.

Jamaal's answer came quickly. "Man, I have done so much damage to God's kids. Yet because of what I have done and the places Jesus has led me to, God is saving more and more kids. I just don't really know how to deal with it."

*   *   *

Father looked over at Peter and said, "This is where I put it on his heart to go back to the ghetto and start working to get those kids to start seeking me to fill the hole in their heart. The enemy has beat up my kids for way too long. We are going to start kickin' his butt all over the place, and in the end, I will send him to hell. Jamaal will be critical to my kingdom in the time he has left in doing just that."

Pete looked over at the great I Am and asked, "What do you mean by, 'the time he has left,' Father?"

Father, with love flowing from every part of him, simply said, "Pete, there are some things I will not tell even you. Just know this: I do know what I am doing."

Peter simply said, "Let me guess. If you tell me, it will take the fun out of it?"

Father shook his head and said, "No, Peter. It's like this; some things you just don't need to know."

Eli walked out into the evening warmth; the sun had disappeared. He grabbed his cell phone and called his beloved.

Jill reached for her phone, looked at the caller ID, and said in her most loving tone, "What's up, sweetheart?"

The look on Eli's face could light up the car interior, even on the darkest night, as he said, "Man, with that tone, I am tempted not to ask you this question. But, do you think we could take Herman out for a Blizzard at Lipinski's Dairy Queen, or do you think it's too late?"

The sweetness in Jill's voice carried over to her next statement. "Why don't you just ask him, Mr. Love of My Life?"

Eli responded with a sweet tone of his own. "Put little Herm on."

Little Herman came running down the stairs in his pajamas, smiling as he ran to grab his mom's phone and answered it. "Hi, Dad!" was Herman's quick answer.

Eli responded to his son, "Hey champ! If you're not too tired, your mom and I would like to take you out for a Blizzard tonight at Lipinski's Dairy Queen."

Herman responded, "Dad, really? That would be fun! I think Mr. Lipinski is great too."

Fifteen minutes later, Eli pulled into the parking lot. Herman and Jill were waiting for him. From their parking lot, they could see the sun starting to sink into the ocean. Eli put his arm around Jill's small waist, kissed her on the cheek, and said. "Babes, what have I done to deserve a life like this?"

Thumbnail jumped onto Jill's shoulder and was about to whisper something into her ear when he heard the Father say in one of his most intense voices. "Thumbnail, this is not the time. You're not needed here." With that, Thumbnail went back to his quarters.

Jill looked at Eli, smiled, and said. "Hun, nothing, except being born. Father knew from the beginning of time what he was going to do with you. You had a choice to follow it or not. But even as a little boy, Father was using you to accomplish great things."

Herman looked up at his mom and dad as the sun was sinking quickly into the ocean. The gulls were flying around the parking lot of the condo, and the tide was making a noise on the beach. He smiled and asked him mom and dad, "Mom, Dad, will I be able to be used by God as much as you guys?"

Eli, with a look of pride on his face that his son would feel the pull to get closer to the Father, simply said, "Christ will use you to the extent that you are willing to surrender to what he wants. Way back when I was your age, my mom's special friend laid hands on me, prayed for me, and I was touched in a way that I just cannot explain. So now, my son, I will pass that onto you." He opened the door of the BMW SUV, grabbed a little olive oil that he had in a grocery bag that he forgot to take in the house. He anointed Herman with the sign of the cross on his forehead and prayed. "Father, touch my son. I pray you will give him the drive to excel at all that he does. Give him the courage to stand for your Word. Make him what you need him to be to accomplish your purpose. In Jesus's name, Amen"

⚾ ⚾ ⚾

Father looked over at Peter. He smiled and stated, "I am going to answer that prayer in such a powerful way that it will blow the socks right off of Jill and Eli."

Peter looked over at the great I Am and said, "Father, what do you have in mind for little Herman?"

The Father gave a slight chuckle as he spoke, "Pete, who makes the sun shine? Who created every star? Who makes the grass green? And who makes the pretty girls' eyes sparkle when they smile?"

Pete had a two word answer to Father's questions. "You do."

Father responded, "Then why do you even question me with what I have in mind? Just accept that it will be a great thing."

⚾ ⚾ ⚾

Herman walked up to his dad as the sun was starting to dip down toward the ocean. He had a question that had been on his mind all day long. The warmth of the evening brought comfort to all those who were sitting outside enjoying the warm smell of the salt coming off the ocean. Herman walked up to Eli and asked him a question, "Dad, I hear in three months that Jamaal gets out of jail. Will I get to meet him then?"

Eli got a surprised look on his face, looked over at Jill as if to say, "Help me, Babes!" Jill smiled back, as if to say, "You're on your own." Eli looked into the eyes of his son. "Tell me, son, why would you want to meet Jamaal?"

Herman looked at his loving father. "Dad, Jamaal has spent almost all of my life behind bars. I have seen him play ball hundreds of times. Mom would get me in the car and bring me home as soon as the game was over. He has served his time. I just want to meet him."

Eli got a huge smile on his face and replied, "My son, so you shall."

Herman's next question was immediate. "When do I get to meet him, Dad?"

Eli, feeling totally challenged by his son, started to become agitated as he answered, "When his sentence is served, we will arrange it. Now, son, it's time for you to hit the sack; it's big day tomorrow and another big game." Eli walked Herman to his room and listened to him pray and kissed him good night.

◍ ◍ ◍

The Father had Hannah sitting on his lap. She had a bit of a tear running down her cheek. "Father, I wish I had gotten to know my dad. He seems like a really nice man."

The great I Am pulled Hannah close to himself and compassionately stated, with a tear running down His face, "When the time is right, you shall."

16
The Right Time

IT'S BEEN TEN years since Jamaal was convicted of selling meth to minors. He was sitting in his cell for the last time in quiet solitude, praying about his future. Unbeknownst to him, in his last games, scouts for Los Angeles have been watching him at Eli's request.

◊ ◊ ◊

The Father looked down on Jamaal sitting in his cell and spoke to Peter, "Pete, you're about to see what I do with individuals, such as Sam and Eli, who achieve greatness and give all the credit to me. Jamaal has served me well in the places he found himself. Like Joseph, he used the time to study and reach those who were serving the sentence for the crimes they committed. Now all of his study is going to come into play. In the future, I will use Jamaal to touch kids. Kids, my kids, are going to have a love for this gentle giant. He will be a huge star! There will be action toys, and every toy will have a cross around its neck.

Kids are going to listen to his teaching and watch him hit home runs."

Peter looked at Father as a tear ran down his cheek. Peter commented, "Father, with all that you do, I should not be amazed. That's what you do, but I am always amazed by you."

🔵 🔵 🔵

The new young jailer came up to the door. "Jamaal, the time of your freedom has come." He put the key in the door, and the giant steps to walk out.

"No, young man, I have been free for years. I am just walking into the continued ministry that the Father has for me."

He walked to the door, and the cutest nine-year-old he could imagine ran up to him, threw his arms around him, and said, "Mr. Jamaal, Mommy and Daddy have talked about you for years. They said I would be able to meet you on this day. I have wanted to meet you and get to know you. I hear you are almost as great a hitter as my daddy is a pitcher."

Jamaal looked down at the boy with warmth that would touch the young boy's very spirit. "And who might your daddy be, little boy?" Jamaal asked with softness and gentleness.

"My daddy is Eli McBrien," the little boy stated with pride.

Eli and Jill stepped out from around the corner. Jill ran up and threw her arms around Jamaal. Eli smiled and said, "Hey man, time to get on with the rest of your life."

With that, Jon Goldsmith stepped out of the car that had been sitting across the street.

Jamaal looked over and saw Mr. Goldsmith walking toward him. He saw the baseball designs on his shirt.

Mr. Goldsmith told him, "Jamaal, you need a job. I am here to offer you one."

Jamaal got a puzzled look on his face. "What kind of a job? Sweeping the stands after a game? I'll take it!"

Jon smiled, "No, not that at all. We want you in center field. We can see you as our next big hitter."

"Does that mean I am going from church league to big league in one step?" Jamaal asked Mr. Goldsmith.

Jon smiled and remarked, "That's exactly what it means!"

Jamaal's response was immediate, "I'll take it!"

Mr. Goldsmith's reply was quick, "You don't even know how much we are going to pay you."

He realized that Herm was still holding his hand and smiling broadly. He looked down and picked the youngster up and placed him on his shoulders. "How much?" was the question returned.

"We are going to pay you the minimum of five hundred thousand dollars a year with a fifty thousand-dollar signing bonus."

"We do have a morals clause. If you associate with any drug dealers, you're out," Mr. Goldsmith added.

"When do I start?" Jamaal asked.

Mr. Goldsmith responded, "Tonight. We just lost Simpson for the season when he fell and broke his leg chasing a fly."

Then Jamaal signed the contract.

That night, as he walked onto the field, he saw the crowd, heard the music over the loud speaker, the Holy Spirit touched him in a way that he had never felt before. Jamaal walked out, understanding that the Father really was in control of everything, and he had taken him from dirt to gold.

Jamaal's thoughts went back to that day when Jill and Eli made that 'wrong turn' into the ghetto. Then his thoughts went to his being busted on meth charges.

"Jamaal, let's go, buddy," Eli said as he walked out with the pitchers. Jamaal snapped out of it, focused on the game ahead, and ran out to center field.

The national anthem played.

LA was playing Frisco. Mark Anderson, their best power hitter, was up to bat. Thomas was pitching, and on the first pitch, Anderson got hold of the ball and drove it to deep center. Jamaal saw the ball leave the bat, go two hundred feet into the air, and go over his head. Jamaal turned and ran back to try and keep under the ball. He saw the ball coming over his shoulder, like a pass from a great quarterback to his receiver, stuck out his glove, and made a great catch over the shoulder grab.

Then he heard Thumbnail. "Jamaal, God has placed you here for the same reason he put Eli into baseball, to reach kids."

Jamaal turned and threw the ball back to second base, and the second baseman relayed it back to Thomas.

The next two outs are accomplished by a strike out and a hard hit ball to the shortstop.

Jamaal walked into the dugout, saw Eli, and asked, "Can I ask you a question?"

Eli responded, "Sure."

Jamaal, with a curious look on his face, inquires, "Ever hear a little voice in your head? I heard one right after I caught that fly ball."

Eli understood what was going on. "Ahhh, what did you hear?"

"I heard that all this was given to me to reach kids," was Jamaal's quick response.

Eli knew exactly what was happening. He knew where those words were coming from. "When you get home tonight, I want you to go on the internet. Go to YouTube and listen to a song by Michael W. Smith called 'Secret Ambition.' It will help you to understand what is happening here."

"Jamaal, you're on deck!" was the word from the manager. Jamaal shook his head, realizing he has to get into this game. He walked to the batter's box, his exuberance showed in his smile. He looked around and saw the thousands of fans smiling down on him. The ump asked, "You gonna bat or just look around?"

He got into the batter's box. At times, over the years playing in the church league, he had to try and hit Eli's balls, so he knew what a fast pitch really looked like. He looked at Rutkers, the Frisco pitcher.

Rutkers thought to himself, *I got this guy. He ain't never gonna see this.* He wound up and threw a fast ball at about 105 mph. Jamaal saw it coming, connected, and sent it out of the park. Home run!

He ran the bases with hands raised in a worshipful manner. The crowd could hear him saying over and over again, "Praise the Lord! Praise Jesus! Praise the God of Jacob! Praise the Lord!"

After rounding the bases, he ran to the dugout, grabbed Eli, and gave him a huge hug.

⚾ ⚾ ⚾

The Father looked at Peter. "Sometimes my work takes years to get to the point where that moment, that second of greatness, comes blasting out of the gate in all of my glory. But my glory always comes out in a way that draws people to me."

The Father looked at Thumbnail, who was as excited as ever jumping up and down on Jamaal's shoulder and said, "What brings me joy is when my kids and yes, even my littlest angel get so excited when My glory shines through one of my other servants.

⚾ ⚾ ⚾

At the press conference after the game, Jamaal was at the podium. The reporters were asking questions.

The tough question came first. "Jamaal, you spent ten years in a county jail. During that time, you have been able to reach kids to keep them off of drugs. Today, you started a new page in your life. How is that going to impact the kids you have been trying to reach?"

Jamaal had a look of sadness and repentance on his face. Thumbnail told Jamaal, "Be honest, tell the world what you have done. Then tell the world what Christ did in you. Give the glory to our Father, who gives new life."

Jamaal looked down at the reporters. "What I have to tell you is going to make some of you hate me, but hopefully, over the years to come, I can make a difference in kids' lives. When I was seventeen, I was in a gang in Watts. I was making a lot of money selling meth, and I did not care who I sold it to. Eli McBrien, with his beautiful wife, Jill, made a wrong turn into the ghetto one day. That was the day Jesus first touched my life. There were several events that took place for me to see there is a better way. That way is our Father in heaven's way. But the loss of life that came from what I was doing should have put me in prison for the rest of my life. I sold meth to a ten-year-old and it killed him. I cannot bring him back. My heart breaks every day that I live, thinking of the damage that I have done, and the lives that I have destroyed. I have been set free from that life of sin. I have been put in a place to make a difference in kids' lives; and with the help of my Father in heaven, through his Son, Jesus, by his Spirit, I will be able to do that."

The reporter asked a follow-up question about the home run.

Jamaal's answer was quick and to the point. "That home run was the Father showing His glory through a hit. I will seek to give Him the glory for every hit I make through the rest of my time here. But the important thing we need to keep in mind is this: we are here only for a season, then we are gone. We have to make a difference in people's lives around us while we are here. I intend to work with all the strength my Heavenly Father gives me to make that difference. And I encourage you to do so as well."

As Jamaal walked out of the stadium, the crowds were huge. Out of the crowd, a woman, the mother of another young boy, walked up to Jamaal and started to pound his chest, "You beast! You damned beast! You killed my son, you beast! You may not have been the one who sold him the drugs that killed him, but you killed him."

Jamaal dropped to his knees and started to sob. "Please forgive me. That is all I can say! Please forgive me!"

Thumbnail jumped over to her shoulder and whispered to her, "Your son did not die in vain. Father has changed this man's heart; he will do much to keep children, such as your son, off of meth. It's time to trust our Father in heaven. Your son is in the presence of the Father. He knows it does not make up for your loss, but Father will make sure he has not died in vain."

She heard Thumbnail loud and clear, and tears began to well up in her eyes. She cried as she said, "I cannot forgive you for what you have done, I just can't. You were an evil man. God may have changed your heart, but you did evil and destructive things."

Father looked at Peter and said, "I have given mothers a love for their children that cannot be broken. Even when a child dies and I bring their spirit here, part of that child stays with the mom. There is a price to be paid for evil that one does; by having 150-year sentence stayed for ten years in the county jail, that boy's mom does not feel justice was done. Jamaal will never have a son of his own. His name will die with him. I will also strike her heart with the prayer that my son taught. You know, the 'Forgive us our sin as we forgive those who sinned against us.' She knows the pain I felt when they killed my Son, the Christ."

Peter cried.

Eli walked up to the lady and touched her shoulder. She turned to see who it was and wrapped her arms around his neck and wept like a baby.

"How do I forgive him?" she asked in tears. "I don't know who sold my son the drugs that killed him. But it could have been him. I don't know who did it. "

The gentle answer came from Eli. "You don't. You have to let the Father forgive him through you. Ma'am, what was your son's name?"

Mrs. Jackson tells Eli her son's name and then said, "Mr. McBrien, you were my little boy's favorite pitcher. He said you believed in Jesus, just like he did."

"Mrs. Jackson, I am honored. Would you like to meet my son?"

Mrs. Jackson smiled. "Yes, I would."

Eli looked over at Jill and motioned to her, and she came over with Herman.

Eli whispered to Mrs. Jackson, "What's your first name?"

"Sharon," she replied.

"Herm, this is our new friend, Sharon Jackson."

Herm said, "Pleased to meet you, Mrs. Jackson."

Sharon got a huge smile on her face.

Jamaal came walking up. Herm ran to him and said, "Mr. Jamaal, can you do something to make Mrs. Jackson feel better?"

Thoughts flooded Jamaal's mind. He told himself, *Let me see what I can do.*

Jamaal walked over to Sharon. "I know I cannot change what I have done, I do not know if I sold drugs to your son or not. But this I know, you have been hurt as well. Here's what I can do. We will give him a living memorial."

Jamaal called the front office and told them of the plan. He would keep the sign-on bonus and three thousand dollars per month. The rest of the money goes to the 'House of Restoration.'"

Sharon asked. "What is the House of Restoration going to be?"

Jamaal somberly answered, "It's going to be a place where young kids, who get caught up in drugs, have a chance to get off. I can't bring him back, but maybe this can be my penance."

Jamaal thought back to the day the judge stayed his 150 years in prison for ten years of jail time and being out of jail to tell kids to stay off drugs and help with the church league baseball. Jamaal heard the words of Thumbnail in his ears. "Dude, you're going to make a lot of money in your life. You will get enough money to sustain yourself, the rest you do not need. But those young lives who were destroyed by people, who have done what you did, can benefit from your contributions."

Eli walked up to him. "What is going through your head, my friend?"

Jamaal responded, "Eli, I am going to make huge amounts of money in this game, and it will all go to the program."

Eli just nodded. He realized it was better not to say anything.

The rest of the season went by in a blur. The management of LA called Jamaal into the office.

The owner of the Dodgers asks him bluntly, "Jamaal, I hear you're still living in low-income housing just outside the ghetto. Why? This team has an image to maintain. Our star center fielder, 'living in the ghetto' does not do that."

Jamaal answered almost shamefully, "Sir, it's all I can afford. All but a few thousand a month go into the House of Restoration."

The owner shook his head and asked, "What is the big deal about that home?"

Jamaal's answer is equally as shameful. "A little red-headed boy died because of what I sold him. This home was set up because of that. The reason I eat most of my meals in the cafeteria is because I don't keep much money for food."

The owner got a look on his face that said, "I will fix this." "Jamaal, I am going to extend your contract and give you a five-year deal worth ten million dollars. You should be able to keep enough of that to provide for yourself."

Jamaal signed the contract, then has the legal document brought forward, signs it, and gives it to the accountant for LA. The document states Jamaal gets fifty thousand dollars a year and the rest goes to the house. Jamaal walks out, and the chief financial officer stops

Jamaal. Here's the sign-on bonus we owe you. We wrote it into the contract, which you did not read, that states the sign-on bonus has to be used on your housing. Get into a good neighborhood. Start working with the kids and help keep the gangs out."

Three years pass, Herman is now twelve and showing the same signs of greatness that his father did at that time.

Jamaal has invested enough money into the House of Restoration and set up a trust fund that would fund it forever. He has spent the last three years pouring directly into the House all the endorsement money he has received from the companies he has shot advertisements for. The little redheaded boy's mom has been placed on the board of directors and has a direct say in how the house is run.

Peter looked over at the Father and asked, "Father, will Herman be able to throw as fast as Eli was able to?"

"No!" was the Father's instant response. "When I said no one would be as great a pitcher as Eli, I meant it. Herman will be a great slugger. His passion is turning those great infield double plays. He will have setbacks and heartbreaks, but in the end, my greatness will shine forth."

It's been a long summer of little league baseball for Herman. He has pounded the ball over and over again. He stole bases with his quickness. And even at this young age, the speed he was able to throw the ball so quickly for the double play almost caught the baseman off guard. Whenever he wants to work overly hard, Eli says, "No! I am not going to have you wreck your arm and lose a career at an early age. Our Father has plans for you young man. For me, those plans meant I was out of baseball early. I understand His wisdom in the way he had things work. I really don't think that is what he has in mind for you."

"Father, Eli really does hear you quite well, does he not?" Peter asked.

"Pete, Herman won't be the pitcher his dad was, but his ministry will be even greater. I put Eli in the ghetto; I am going to use Herman to bridge the rich and the poor. I am going to use Herman to be a messenger of mine throughout his career and beyond."

Herman came running down the steps. "Dad, are you going to be at my game today? It's for the City Championship. If we win this, then we get to compete for the Little League World Series."

The answer from Eli was immediate and exciting. "I would not miss it! I hear you pitched to a few of the LA team at practice yesterday?"

Herman came into the room with a huge smile on his face. "Did Jamaal tell you I pitched to him?"

Eli's smiled greatly. "Yeah, and the change up I taught you caught him completely off guard. You struck him out.

It kinda makes me wish you liked pitching more than play-ing shortstop. But it's your game and not mine. But Jamaal did tell me he had almost the same trouble hitting you as he did me. Maybe, just maybe, you could pitch relief once in a while."

Herman smiled even a bigger smile as he said, "Dad, I know I can pitch. The problem is, I would rather play shortstop. It's more fun for me. I love turning the double plays. I will pitch if the team gets into a jam. The one thing you taught me was that the team comes above all else when I am on the field. Dad, I really do think that the Father would rather use me at shortstop."

⚾ ⚾ ⚾

The Father looked over at his Son, Jesus. "Son, you created joy in victory, and that joy sure came out in Herman.

Jesus looked at the Father and smiled as broadly, if not more so than Herman.

⚾ ⚾ ⚾

Just then, Eli's cell phone rang. It was Sam.

⚾ ⚾ ⚾

Thumbnail was standing before the Father. "Father, I did all that I could do. I screamed at him not to go into the ghetto. He would not listen to me."

⚾ ⚾ ⚾

Eli answered his cell. "Sam buddy, what's happenin'?"

Eli's face turned white, and tears start to well up in his eyes. "Nooo!" was all that Eli could say. Eli forced a smile and told Herm to go inside with his mom. Herm hesitated. Eli demands with more intensity, "NOW!" Herman, not hearing his father raise his voice often, did as he was told.

"Okay, Sam, what happened?" asked Eli. The voice on the other end of the line was shaky, like someone who was terribly hurt.

"Eli, I cannot understand it. I have no idea why he would go back to the ghetto. He knew that his life was not worth a plugged nickel there after he turned States evidence on all the drug lords down there. The team is covering all of his final expenses, but it is devastating to his mom."

Eli walked to his BMW, got in, and cried like a baby. He composed himself and asked, "Father, I don't have to understand why, but would you show me what I need to say to Herm? He was just getting to know Jamaal."

○ ○ ○

The Father motioned to Thumbnail. "Thumbnail, I want you back on Eli's shoulder. When he talks to his son, you tell him exactly what he needs to say."

○ ○ ○

Eli walked into their house. Jill walked up to him, put her arms around him, and asked, "Eli, what was that all about? Herm told me you raised your voice at him."

Eli responded with tears in his eyes. "Jill, this game is really important for Herm. If I tell you what this was about, Herm may see it on your face. Trust me, when the time is right, I will tell you."

Jill looked and smiled at Eli. Then she put her arms around him and whispered, "Eli McBrien, I really do love you."

They were able to put on a happy face as they went out to the ball park. Herm reminded Eli of himself. Time after time he would grab a grounder and get the ball to first in a second. Time after time he got closer and closer to the final inning. He threw out the final runner then walked off the field, threw his arms around his mom and dad. "Hey folks, you think this has earned me a DQ tonight?" As they walked into Lipinski's Dairy Queen, Herm ordered his favorite meal and a peanut buster parfait. He smiled as he enjoyed every last bit of it.

Herman noticed that his dad, however, seemed to be almost crying all night.

He asked in his gentle voice, "Dad, what's wrong?"

Eli looked over at Herman. Thumbnail started to whisper into Eli's ear.

"Herm, when Jamaal was young, he did some very bad things. He wanted to stop, but things caught up with him. For him not to spend the rest of his life in jail, he had to turn state's evidence on all of his so-called-friends who were selling drugs. For some reason, last night he went back to the ghetto, and they killed him. Herm, there is a lesson to be learned. Actually, a couple of them; one, as Paul states, bad company is the ruin of good morals.

You can do all the good in the world, but your past will come back to haunt you. Christ paid the price for our sin, but what we have done on this earth will be paid for on this earth. Second, if we build a positive reputation, one built on integrity, that will follow us all of our lives as well. Now you have a job to do. I know this is a shock to your system, but you have to shake it off and walk in what Father has created you to do. Ask yourself, what is your secret ambition?"

Herman walked into his room and put his Michael W. Smith CD into his player. He laid on his bed, put his headphones on, and turned up the volume. He heard the drums, the runs on the guitar, and knew what his secret ambition was for the next game at least. He listened to the song a couple of times and decided it was time to go to sleep. When his mom peeked in and saw him on the bed, she told him it was time to go to sleep.

Three days later, Herman found himself playing short-stop against a bunch of kids from Chicago to see who would go to Japan for the Little League World Series. He watched as the pitcher threw against Chicago. He would cut off ball after ball and get the ball to first, or throw to second for the double play. Then it hit him. His team needed him to pitch. When the inning was over, he walked up to his coach and told him what he really felt needed to be done. The coach smiled. He had been waiting for Herman to come to that conclusion. The coach pulled Johnson, the pitcher, and put Herman in for his first pitching assignment.

Thumbnail whispered to him, "Remember, Herman, not by might, nor by power, but by my Spirit, says the Lord."

Herman looked around, not understanding where those words were coming from. He took the ball, flipped it from behind up over his shoulder and into a waiting glove. He smiled at the batter. He winked, wound up, and threw the ball at a respectful 85 mph. The batter was not even close to hitting the ball. All of a sudden, he heard the drums, the runs on the guitar, and he was in the zone. He knew his secret ambition. He sensed that Jamaal was watching with God and smiling down on him. He threw faster and faster and struck out hitter after hitter.

Eli looked at Jill. She appeared as excited as when she used to watch him pitch. He smiled to himself, knowing who is really in control of this thing.

Herman's little league team would win their trip to the World Series The new chapter in the Father's move to touch kids would continue as a new hero was created. Something became clear as the story continued: the Father was looking down on Herman, and he had his back. So Herman's greatness became the glory of our Father.

And the glory of the Father is passed to the Son by the Spirit.

The Father looked over at Peter, smiled, and said, "As I passed my greatness to the Christ at his resurrection, Eli is passing to Herman his greatness. So the next book that is going to be written is of this young lad. With every person, there is a story. Most people aren't aware of the impact they could have on those around them, but for the person who is willing, I will do great things. Watch, as Herman receives my greatness and touches those around him in a greater way than his father."

Peter responded, "Father, you said he won't be as great a pitcher as his father?"

Father answered in his loving voice, "Peter, the lives he touches will be millions. The lives his father touched were hundreds. That, my son, is true greatness. Watch, as I take the greatness that is passed from Eli to Herman and multiply it. You will see what happens with Herman McBrien as he receives the greatness of Eli. Herman will receive the greatness passed on to him."